DELIVERANCE OF
SARA

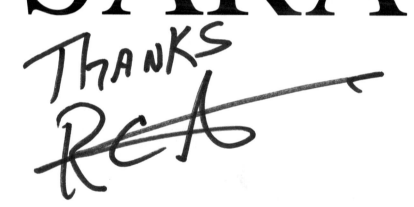

Thanks

RCA

CONTACT THE AUTHOR
RCJAMES@VALORNET.COM

DELIVERANCEOFSARA.COM

Thanks
RC

DELIVERANCE OF SARA

R.C. James

Aventine Press

Published by Aventine Press
750 State St. #319
San Diego CA, 92101

ISBN: 1-59330-550-8

Library of Congress Control Number: 2008934543
Library of Congress Cataloging-in-Publication Data
Deliverance Of Sara

Printed in the United States of America

Prologue

The following story is true, I know; I was there for much of it. The story may read stranger than any fiction, but every word is truth. It has not been an easy decision for me to put this story out for public consumption. Over the years I have shared the intriguing events with a select few; digging out my notes and tapes, telling as gently as I could the events of that time far away in the remote mountains of Mexico. I now feel it is time for all to come to the knowledge of the truth about a side of life that we seemingly all know is there, but to which we are reluctant to open our minds.

As a young man I trained as a reporter and worked in that field, both domestically and on assignment in Vietnam. I decided to use strict investigative reporting criteria in describing this disturbing string of events. All events written about were either experienced by me personally, witnessed and related to me by at least two persons, or related to me by a single person who had proven to be extremely reliable through my past experiences with them. I interviewed each person, took notes, and/or made recordings to keep my recollections true to the events. In the interest of decency I have softened some of the sexual abuses of the young lady that was at the center of those horrific events, but by reading between the lines the reader will be able to understand the baseness and evil to which many in this world are subjected. It is certainly not my intention to offend, but only to inform. Those events are true and are a relevant part of the evils perpetrated. The timeline is accurate, but the year dates have not been shown; and the names of individuals and places have been changed to protect the privacy of those who were the victims of the horrors, and of those who opened up their hearts to help with the reconstruction of the events.

Understand that after you have read this book you will never look at the world in quiet the same manner. You will see the love of God for His creation. You will see how so many events in our lives are of the handy work of the Creator, and you will come to understand that many of those things might have just been considered coincidences. You will also realize the depth of the grace of God, and at the same time you will see the depth of evilness on the dark side, that part of our world controlled by Lucifer and his minions. Yes, there is magnificent good in this universe, but there is also the diametrically opposed.

NEVER DOUBT THIS: THERE IS EVIL OUT THERE AND IT IS AFTER YOU. IT IS AFTER YOU TO DESTROY YOU AND AFTER YOUR FAMILY TO DESTROY THEM!

1 Peter 5:8 "Be sober, be vigilant; because your adversary the devil walks about like a roaring lion, seeking whom he may devour." (NKJV of the Holy Scriptures)

Chapter One

Just after sunset, April 18th in San Mateo, a remote village in the Sierra Madre Oriente Mountains, Mexico.

Even though it was early evening and not too long after sunset, the darkness of this night was suffocating. The only noticeable light in the entire area was the occasional lightning from a storm in the distance, so far in the distance that the thunder claps could not be heard. As the lightning spider-webbed across the sky in an eerie display of the wrath of Mother Nature, the village of San Mateo could barely be seen in the otherwise pitch-blackness. San Mateo is an "Ejido" which is an area of land owned equally by all who lived there. Those living there were "Mestizos," a proud, hearty people with a mixed ancestry of Indian, Spanish, and French. Though the village had been in existence in one form or another for hundreds of years, it had been officially established as an "Ejido" after the uprising of Pancho Villa in the first part of the twentieth century. In that revolution, the peasant population rebelled against the rich landowners and divided the spoils of the land amongst themselves. Operating as a quasi-commune, with some intermingling private ownership, This small section of land and its approximately two hundred inhabitants had survived poverty, drought, civil wars, corrupt governments, bandits, outlaws, smugglers, and spiritual evilness for over three centuries.

The village consisted of twenty-four families living on the side of a 13,000 ft. mountain known as Jefe Mountain. The illumination created by the lighting was scarce at best, but the shapes of the huts could be discerned. The huts were constructed, as were most all dwellings in these small villages throughout the mountains, with sticks, mud, and thatch. The walls of sticks were held together with strips of the thatch material made from the palm-like leaves of a local plant called "suate"; then mud "adobe" was smeared on the outside of the sticks as a sealant. The roofs were fashioned out of sticks and covered over with the thatch material. The huts were exceedingly small and flimsy due to the construction and the materials used for that construction. An occasional stronger and more durable mud brick building might appear among the other structures, but these were the exception and not the rule. Because of the design and the building materials, the huts were small, usually not over one hundred and fifty square feet, and most were even smaller.

The families generally used one hut for cooking and eating and another as a sleeping area for the whole family. On rare occasions or in the instance of larger families, more than one sleeping hut would be utilized. There might even be a storage hut if the family so desired and could afford the luxury of another structure. The beds were corn shucks piled on the dirt floor with a thin hand-made horsehair blanket placed on top of the shucks to serve as bedding. To keep warm during the cool or sometimes even cold nights, another horsehair blanket would be used for cover. Around each pair or group of huts stood a stick fence, usually constructed of rocks gathered from nearby, designating the family's property and containing the animals: goats, pigs, dogs, chickens, horses, and mules.

There was no electricity, running water or sewage facilities. San Mateo, as with many other villages in these remote mountains, was a time-warp to the mid-1800s, akin to the Old West in the United States. A road, more accurately described as a trail wound up the mountain to the village, but no one in the village owned a vehicle. Travel was accomplished by walking or by riding horseback or utilizing the many mules and donkeys. Many of these people had never been out of these mountains, had never seen a television, ate in a restaurant, or rode in a car. The diet included beans, cactus, eggs, and corn tortillas, with the occasional chicken; all foodstuffs were grown or raised by the villagers locally. Water was carried in buckets from a spring about a quarter-mile up the side of Jefe Mountain from the village. The clothes, including shoes, were for the most part hand made, designed for function only. It was a poverty stricken life, but the villagers did not realize the difficulty of their lives as it was the only way of life they had ever known.

San Mateo was typical of the villages in this remote part of mountainous Mexico, but there was definitely something not typical about this particular night. At this hour on any other evening, the village would be buzzing with activity. The women would be cooking, the men bedding down their animals, and the children would be being children by dodging chores, running, and playing. Illumination from the cooking fires would be emanating from each of the cooking huts, and there would be a steady din of sound from all the activity. Sounds from the people and the animals, especially from the many dogs, would normally be echoing throughout the village; large dogs, small dogs, and dogs of all types would be barking and baying at every movement and shadow. They carried on all night, every night. They would seemingly take shifts sleeping, so there would be no time of silence. This night was different. The dogs were absolutely silent. The families had gone into their sleeping huts without eating or even caring for or bedding down their animals. They huddled beneath their meager horsehair covers, not speaking or moving, fearful of making any noise. For the most part they kept their eyes shut, but when they were opened they reflected the fear that resided within all the residents of San Mateo. This night was *"una noche de esperituales" (night of the spirits)*. The darkness was complete, the silence was deafening, and as the lightning increased in intensity across the distant sky there was only one barely noticeable exception.

On the highest side of the village, one hut displayed some evidence of activity. Through the cracks in the wall and around the entryway, small streams of yellowish light stood out against the otherwise utter darkness. The light came from the burning wood that was on the open cooking hearth and from a few small, homemade candles. Outside of the hut, two very large dogs huddled beneath a woodpile. They were shivering, not from cold, but rather from fear; a fear that they did not understand. The fear had overcome them quietly and suddenly as the last rays of sunlight turned orange, then red, and finally dimmed in the west. These dogs, which had taken on mountain lions and black bears as part of their responsibility of guarding the goatherds, were now frightened beyond description by something they could not see or hear, something in the darkness. The dogs as well as all the other residents of San Mateo, animal and human, knew something was amiss. No one had to tell them that an evil, an extreme evil, was present in their normally peaceful village. They just knew. The dogs whimpered and shivered and the families huddled together and waited for the rising of the sun. They waited for those first rays of sun to purify the village and chase away the darkness that housed the unseen and unspeakable terror in their midst.

Inside of the small hut, the only one that was showing any light, were eight souls. In the interior of the meager hut opposite the cooking hearth area were two men who sat on sections of hand hewed logs that served as chairs. It was Juan Soto, the owner of the hut, and a guest,. The owner Juan was typical of the mountain dwellers of his time. He was small, strong, and his skin appeared weatherworn from years of hard work in the sun. Juan had no formal education, was nearly illiterate, and he lived from meal to meal, day to day, just trying to survive. His poverty showed in his attire, his wrinkled scarred hands, his speech, and his actions. The other man, Juan's guest, was known only as Xanateo (Haan' a taeo). Xanateo was a Warlock.

Xanateo was a full-fledged Satan worshipping, spell casting, God hating, twisted, perverted, controlling, and evil Warlock. His attire showed his affluence, as he wore store-bought clothes and had socks on under his fancy lace-up shoes. His face was not weatherworn and his smooth hands sported many gold rings, most with strange designs of snakes, spiders, and other satanic symbols. These rings were of a type which Juan Soto had never seen before. The dissimilarity of the two men could not have been more extreme. In Juan's hand were four, two peso gold coins (worth in total about $60.00 U.S.). This was much more money than Juan had ever seen at one time in his entire life. Xanateo had given the elderly villager the four coins as payment for the youngest daughter in the Soto family.

The negotiations had been going on for nearly three months. Xanateo had assured the Soto family that no harm would befall their young daughter. He told them that she had 'the gift' and that all he and his group wanted was to teach and train her in the ways of the spirits. He promised that the daughter would be kept pure, unharmed, and be returned to them in two years. She would be home before her fifteenth birthday and would be the pride and joy of the family, and of the entire village. At that time, when all of the villagers recognized the knowledge that Juan's daughter, Sara, would have obtained, they would give much respect to her; and even more to Juan Soto. In the mind of Juan Soto, these promises served as a source of great pride and honor to the family. After the deal had been struck, a series of ritual baths were performed on the girl; tonight was the final ceremony, the seventh ritual cleansing bath. The ritual was taking place on the other side of a crude curtain, made from some tattered clothes and horsehair blankets, which kept the men separated from the women and the young girl. As the men talked in hushed tones, the women were carrying out their duties with great purpose.

On the women's side of the partition, standing around the small, wooden horse-watering trough that had been brought inside to act as a bathing tub, were five women. The mother of the girl and four Witches from the Coven of Xanateo huddled around the young girl, who sat in the makeshift ritual tub. The Witches were Santiaga, Brillintina, Josefa, and Magdelena, and they had all came into the Coven by the same ritual they were performing tonight for the youngest child of Juan Soto. All had served Xanateo for many years and were quite proficient in their duties. They worked with what could be called obsessive fervor and with great expectation of things to come. Things to come of which, at the present time, only they were privy; things that were only whispered about by the ill-informed. The mother stood by, moving only when she was instructed to do so by one of the Witches, not daring to look them in the eyes due to a fear of something that she did not comprehend.

Sara had reached her puberty a short three months earlier and her body was just beginning to show the blossoming of a young woman. She was shaking, nervous, and afraid; she was also completely and totally embarrassed. Her mother had administered the other six baths, but now she was naked in front of strangers. She had never before been naked in front of anyone except her mother and now there was a room full of people. Deep inside, she felt something stirring, stirrings caused by the attention, the promises that everyone would admire her when she came back, and the power or even authority that she had felt at times since the bathing rituals had begun. She felt stirrings insider her that she had never before imagined. It seemed to her that these people were at least somewhat concerned about what or who she was, and all she had to do was stay with these seemingly nice folks and learn the ways of the spirits, or "Brujeria" (witchcraft). No more herding goats or carrying water or working in the fields. She would do whatever they asked in expectation of an easier life, and to keep experiencing the stirrings that were occurring deep inside her.

The Witches had given Sara a pain-numbing and hallucinogenic herb, and after the effects of the drug set in, Santiaga and Josefa massaged all of Sara's body with sweet smelling oil soap. They were very careful not to miss any part of her body as they continued massaging. Brillintina brought the hot water that had been heating on the open pit wood cooking area. As they poured the water over the girl as they continued massaging with the oil soap, the lather completely covered Sara, and the room was overwhelmed by the strong fragrances. Magdelena was preparing a small knife for the mutilation sacrifice that would soon take place. She was working with a sacramental obsidian bladed knife, the same type that the Aztec Indians used hundred of years in the past for their human sacrifices. The handle, formed from a human pelvic bone, was in the shape of a coiled snake, and the stone blade was black, shiny and sharper than any scalpel in a modern hospital's surgical room.

As Sara, responding to the instructions, stood and the lather and oil ran off of her body, more water was poured over her and she started to shiver, not from cold, but from something else deep inside her core that she did not understand. Magdelena took the ancient ritual knife and cut a shallow but relatively large pentagram between Sara's small, budding breasts. She administered two cuts to each line of the pentagram, each at a different angle; by doing so the raised scar that was desired would be produced. The pain should have been overwhelming, but the pain-killing herb was at work, and Sara felt hardly anything. The wound bled profusely for a time until sienna powder was rubbed into the freshly made wound.

The bleeding stopped and the small amount of pain Sara had felt started to subside. The triple effect of the sienna powder was to stop the bleeding, color the wound and subsequent scar tissue, and to totally deaden any pain. The outline of the pentagram was now a very dark reddish brown, almost black. When it was completely healed it would leave a raised scar that would be black and permanent. At this juncture Sara was feeling very dizzy from the drugs, and as she watched what was happening to her it was as though it was happening to someone else. As the drugs took full effect she felt no pain, and she was so light-headed that she even giggled occasionally for no apparent reason. She knew that she should be hurting, but there was no pain. She knew she should be really embarrassed, standing naked before these strangers, but now she wasn't, not in the least. She actually felt completely enthralled by all the attention.

After this, Sara was inspected and ministered to by the Witches, who made sure the bleeding had completely stopped and the coloration of the pentagram was sufficient. She was then dressed in the most beautiful dress Sara could ever imagine. Her hair was combed and styled in a way she had never thought possible. The Witches even had a hand mirror so Sara could see herself. She had never used a hand mirror before, only small broken pieces of mirror that she had found or a shiny piece of metal to look at herself. New shoes were put on her feet, real shoes, not the homemade ones to which she had become accustomed. A necklace, with a pendant in the shape of a small jaguar attached, was then clasped around her neck. This was the first piece of jewelry that Sara had ever worn.

Sara was then given another drug potion to drink and instructed to begin repeating the following: "I welcome you, spirit from the great Somne Octe, I welcome you to your new home. I do not resist, I do not resist."

She repeated this over and over for what she thought to be an eternity but in reality was about two hours.

The four Witches surrounded her and repeated, "Somne Octe, Somne Octe, Somne Octe, Somne Octe, Somne Octe," over and over and over.

Somne Octe had been summoned by the faithful in the hut at the high end of the village and he would soon be arriving. Somne Octe was a demon, and not just a run of the mill average everyday demon. He was the commander and controller of this entire mountainous section of Eastern Mexico. He ranked very high in the scheme of things here on earth. In the evil dominions set forth on the earth by the supreme ruler of darkness, he had done well. Only Damien ranked above him in this quadrant, and Damien answered directly to Lucifer himself. Somne Octe had served Prince Lucifer well over the eons of time since the great rebellion and banishment from heaven. He had survived the initial chaos, escaped the chains of damnation, and had been promoted over and over until finally being given complete responsibility for this area of the mountains, which is called the eighth sector. Somne Octe had been elevated to his present level of authority and had controlled these mountains for hundreds of years. Ruling openly with the power of evil; he remained unchallenged from the other side.

Doing as he so desired or was commanded to do by his immediate superior Damien, Somne Octe operated his dominion without opposition from anyone or anything. He did the bidding of the Supreme Evil One as relayed by Damien in total freedom and without any interference from the forces of good. There had never been a serious challenge to his authority, not one. Now some of his very faithful human servants were summoning him and he would not disappoint them. It had already been reported to him that there was going to be a new one added to the faithful this night, and he took this opportunity to bring fear to the village, and through that fear more respect for his faithful servants and himself. He called all the demons and evil spirits who were not in a human or animal host to gather and to celebrate. He commanded them to come, obey, and honor him. He commanded those minions of destruction to gather here on this mountain, on this night, so that chaos, fear, turmoil, and violence would consume all of the village of San Mateo.

When the chanting started in the hut, the air in the rest of the village seemed to thicken to a point that the villagers had to labor to breathe. The babies began to scream at the top of their lungs as the terrified mothers tried to quiet them. In the whole village, with the sole exception of the Soto's compound, the animals were now becoming restless and tearing loose from their ties, running, fighting, and ripping through the village. For no apparent reason the dogs began fighting each other and at the same time trying to break into the small huts. Dust from all the commotion of the animals began to rise and fill the air, making it even harder to breathe. The huts had gone from a place of refuge, a hiding place, to a very poorly fortified place of protection from the animals. The craziness and evil of that night began to manifest in the people as well. Those huddled in the huts began to bicker and blame each other for the events that were taking place. Some of the normally docile men in that normally quite village began screaming at and hitting their wives and children; then, in response, those children began to physically attack each other. The wave of terror and turmoil rolled through the small village like a dark fog.

In one hut, the home of Jeremias Mendes, the fear of the night took a decided turn for the worst as the hoards of demons continued sweeping into town. Jeremias sat in the corner of his hut, ashamed of the fear he felt, but totally consumed by it. In his mind the demons were telling him that his wife, because of the fear he showed, would not respect him in the future. The evil ones repeatedly told him that Juana Mendez, his wife of nearly twenty years, would despise him and become unfaithful to him because of his fear and weakness. A dark and brooding attitude came over Jeremias as he crawled out from under the covers and hit his wife in the face with his doubled up fist. In over twenty years he had not even raised his voice, but now he hit her over and over. He screamed "puta, puta, puta" (whore, whore, whore), and continued to brutally beat Juana. The children cried and begged their father to stop as they pulled at him trying to protect their mother. Then, unexplainably, the children began to hit each other and scream in their loudest voices. Jeremias would have probably killed Juana, and possibly the children, if their mule had not interrupted him. The normally docile animal had crashed through the stick and mud wall of the hut and was kicking at anything and anyone that moved. This danger distracted Jeremias from the demonic drive to beat his wife to death. After turning his attention to the mule, and driving the crazed animal out of the hut, the anger in him subsided. He now felt brave after protecting his family that just moments before he had been trying to destroy. The family again huddled together in extreme terror beneath the blanket and waited for morning and the rays of the rising sun to deliver them.

This type of turmoil was commonplace in the other huts as the demonic spirits planted lies and fears in the minds of the villagers. The village's men, women, children, babies, and animals were all on the verge of insanity. The spiritual attacks became too much for many to bear and they ran blindly from their huts and from the village, not knowing where they were running to, or exactly what they were running from. They just ran and ran until they would fall, exhausted and shaking with fear. Many were injured from falling down steep grades or tripping over rocks and other obstacles in the pitch blackness of the night. It seemed as though every demonic spirit in the Mexico had gathered on the side of Jefe Mountain and invaded this small village, yet it wasn't every demonic spirit in Mexico, it was only those that had been summoned by Somne Octe.

In the Soto's hut, the chanting was at a fever pitch. Sara had her head rolled back and her upper lip was pulled back over her teeth as saliva was running from the corners of her mouth, dripping off the sides of her chin and onto her shoulders. Even though it was very cool inside the hut, beads of perspiration formed on Sara's forehead and upper lip. She had been assured that this was her night that she was being elevated from poor mountain girl to the respected (or more likely feared) status of Bruja. More feelings were stirring inside here that she did not understand, or at the moment care to understand. She also felt a presence that was completely foreign to the experiences of her young life. She thought that what was happening to her was strange, wrong, and even evil but she did not care; she was beginning to welcome the stirrings. After two hours Sara was psychologically overwhelmed by the drugs, the chanting, and the surrounding demonic activity. She began to move her young body to unheard music and totally gave into the feelings rising inside her. Her eyes widened with excitement and anticipation, and her breath came in short gasps. The witches surrounding Sara were in their own trance as they danced in place to the unheard tempo. Groans were escaping the lips of the Witches as the scene devolved into one of seemingly total decadence and chaos, but it wasn't chaos, for the spiritual realm of Somne Octe was carefully orchestrating it.

Sara's mother could do nothing but sit and cry and her father closed his hand on the money, wishing these people would just take his daughter and go away. Just before midnight, Xanateo went to the area of the hut where Sara was and told his witches that it was time. Then he took Sara by the shoulders and looked deeply and intently into her eyes. He instructed her to open her mind, soul, and body to receive the visitor that was about to enter her. Sara's body began to tremble and shake as she did as was instructed. In the spiritual realm, Somne Octe chose one of his minions to move into the warmth and moistness of Sara's body. The demon chosen was a 'familiar spirit,' one that specialized in revealing secrets to humans. Even the deepest and darkest parts of one's life were not privy to this type of evil spirit. This demon, this fallen angel, was used for divination and fortune-telling. This evil spirit was also used to bring trouble, turmoil, and conflict into every area of human life. These divining spirits cannot foretell the future, but when they first reveal to someone the secrets of their past, whatever predictions of the future they make are easily believed by the recipient of those prophecies. The object of this demonic spirit is to steal and destroy, and to bring confusion by combining some truth with a multitude of lies. This evil scheme always works with those who do not have an understanding of the spiritual realm around us, which, sadly, is most of the world's populace. This particular divining spirit was named 'Basar.' In the ancient language of Babylon, the name means "the revealer." Basar had served Somne Octe well over the stretches of time, and was now rewarded with a soft, warm, and moist body to inhabit.

Somne Octe reflected on the events of that night and knew that those above him in the order of things would be pleased, and he would gain much respect from the demons in other sectors. He reflected on his last promotion, many hundreds of years before, with only two superiors in the ranks above him; arrogance and pride rose up in Somne Octe. He felt that someday he would take Damien's place and possibly even, well possibly share the Seat of Satan. Sara was ready to become another faithful servant of the dark side. Somne Octe and Xanateo would both be rewarded for their faithfulness in carrying out the events that would take place this night.

Xanateo instructed Sara to receive her visitor and yield to the forces and desires she felt stirring inside her. He carefully guided Sara to simply trust what was happening, to neither question nor doubt, and to yield totally. Sara's eyes rolled back in her head as she took a deep breath and shuddered to the very core of her young, innocent soul. Basar took up residence in the warmth and comfort of his host. He had been invited in and in he came. It would be much more difficult to move him out than it was to ask him in. No longer walking around in the dry places, he felt at home, and home to stay. He would greatly please his master with as much mayhem as he could conjure among the humans. Somne Octe watched as Basar entered into the young girl. He knew that Basar was only the first of many who would be sent to take up residence in Sara, all in due time. Sara felt the difference immediately, it was not as though anything physical had changed, but she seemed to have more knowledge and a greater understanding of her surroundings. There were also more feelings stirring inside her – deep, sensual feelings that she could not fathom yet. As stated, Sara had only entered puberty a few months earlier and these sensual feelings felt foreign and slightly unsettling to her. However, the drugs were doing their duty, and the unsettling feeling did not last long. It was now midnight and Xanateo was ready to be through with this part of the ceremony.

Xanateo brought Sara to her father and told her to sit across from him. Sara's mother was sent outside while the next part of the ceremony was to take place. Sara sat down where she had been instructed and she sheepishly looked at the floor as it was not the custom for a daughter to stare into the face of her father. She was instructed by one of the Witches, who whispered into her ear, to look her father in the face and to open her mouth, so that Basar could speak through her. Juan Soto sat in disbelief as he stared at the dress, shoes, and jewelry Sara wore. He was wishing he had the money that they cost, thinking it to be a waste of money on this girl. Sara looked at her father and, from somewhere deep inside of her, out through her mouth, came a deep voice, a man's husky voice, commanding and full of authority and power. Her father was visibly shaken by this turn of events; he wanted to run out of the hut, but pride and fear held him. In reality all he wanted was for them to leave him and his money alone.

Basar begin to speak through Sara and to reveal to everyone in the room the secrets of Juan's past. The voice spoke of the infidelity of Juan with a sister of his wife, and of a time he stole money from a brother. The voice coming from his daughter even spoke of a homosexual event one night in the city when Juan was full of 'Pulqe' (a very strong alcoholic drink). Continuing revelation told of stealing neighbors' animals, and the voice from inside of Sara spoke on and on. Juan began to tremble and started begging Xanateo to stop her and to please not tell anyone what was being said. The sweat ran off Juan's face as he nearly passed out from the terror that was rising inside him, overwhelming him, starting to choke him, and eventually completely terrifying him. Xanateo didn't speak a word as he put out his hand, palm up. Juan, continuing to tremble and shake, now sobbed openly. He knew what he must do, and he reluctantly took the four small gold coins and placed them in the waiting hand of Xanateo.

Juan looked at his daughter in disbelief and with hatred as he screamed, "Puta, puta, puta" (Whore, whore, whore). He spit at her before running out of the hut to hide his shame in the suffocating darkness of the night.

Sara felt a rush of excitement that she had never experienced. An older and more experienced woman would recognize it as sexual arousal and gratification, but not this young girl. She had no idea what the feeling was. The group gathered their things and left the hut, disappearing into the night. Xanateo instructed the four Witches to walk on each side and in front of and behind Sara. Xanateo led the small group on the three-hour walk to Lleno, the town where the Witches' Coven House was located; and where the completion of the indoctrination would take place. The Coven House was the place where Sara would begin to realize the true depth of the darkness into which she was being initiated and the evilness into which she had been sold. For now, the drugs, the feeling of power, and those ever-increasing deep strange feelings kept any possible concerns well under control. She was ecstatic with the turn of events in her otherwise dull and drab existence, though unaware of the depths of utter wickedness to which she would be subjected to this very night.

The hoards of demons continued to wreak havoc in the village on the side of Jefe Mountain. It would continue until sunrise and then just as quickly as it had started, it would cease. Some of the older villagers had a vague idea of what was happening; not precisely, but they knew that this night would be the causation of even more evil in the future. They knew that more evil and terror would be coming – maybe not this week, this month, or even this year – but what had started this night was not over. These older ones had seen similar events before and knew that other things would result from the unknown events that had taken place this night. The village would stir and come alive in the advancing early morning light, and not one word of the events of the night before would ever be mentioned. Publicly it would be as though the terror had never happened, while privately the villagers carried the fear and terror deep inside of themselves.

Chapter 2

The group escorting Sara arrived at Santiaga's place of residence, the Witches Coven House, about two-and-a-half hours before sun-up. The plain house sat among the other structures built along the foot of the mountains. The adobe structure was not much different than any other in the larger and slightly more modern town of Lleno. There was a difference, but it could not be seen from the dirt path that ran along the front of the residence. Only from the inside, after removing part of a false wall, could the ceremonial room and its altar be seen. The house had been built with the back against the entrance of a small cave. The cave had been dug and shaped into the mountain to be a completely hidden room. It was a room from which no sound could escape and into which prying eyes could not see.

Xanateo went into the house to rest and ready himself for the completion of the ceremony. Two of the Witches scurried around Sara, getting her ready for another hot bath and fresh clothes. One bruja was working on her hair and the other was doing what ever was necessary to aid in the preparation; checking the effects of the drugs, placing sweet smelling cologne on her, repeatedly telling her everything would be all right, etc. The other two brujas were preparing the ceremonial cave for the completion of the induction. About an hour-and-a-half before sunrise, the Witches took Sara and went into the ceremonial cave. The

Witches were in their customary bright-colored, loose fitting dresses, while Sara was dressed in a white, flowing dress. There was an altar fashioned from a large boulder in the center of the room. The boulder had been in place before the room was created, and it had been chiseled into its present shape when the room was finished.

The altar was three feet high, three feet wide, and six feet long. It had been hand hewn to a semi-rough finish with many sharp and angular edges on the surface. Sara was impressed, astonished even, at the sight of the ceremonial room and the altar. There were four large candles next to the altar itself, at the four cardinal points of the compass. Eight hand-carved, wooden candle stands with four candles on each surrounded the altar, two on each of the four sides. A fire burned on the ground at each of the four corners. The fires glowed with a deep green color caused by soaking the firewood in a solution of copper dust and alcohol prior to the preparation phase. The walls glistened with natural mica and iron pyrite, giving the appearance of a wall that was studded with diamonds and gold. Along with the green fires and white candlelight reflecting off the sparkling walls, the overall effect was no less than spectacular.

Sara was forced to drink more herb mixture, but this time it was berra-berra root and cocaine that was mixed with very potent proof rum. This mixture heightens the senses to an extreme degree, and keeps the mind and body active for long periods of time. They repeatedly gave her more of the potent mixture as they brought her to the base of the altar. Sara was greatly influenced by the drugs as the Witches positioned her close to one of the candle stands so the light would hinder her vision. She tried to move, but the grip of the four older women held her in position. At the other end of the cave-room, on the other side of the candles, a figure moved. Sara could not make out who it was or what it was. It looked human, but again it didn't.

Xanateo stood in the semi-darkness at the edge of the cave-room. He was extremely affected by the drugs he had been ingesting and smoking. He had been drinking berra-berra root mixed with cocaine and rum, and had also injected himself with a mixture of cocaine and yahimbe, the latter being a very potent aphrodisiac. He stood in the shadows, his breathing labored, and his eyes wide with the drugs, and with anticipation. He started to walk slowly towards Sara. What Sara saw drove her to the edge of insanity. She saw an animal, an animal unlike any she had ever seen. It looked like a man, but it was an animal, a goat; a goat with two legs.

Xanateo's only covering was prepared especially for these inductions. He had fashioned the skull of a ram, complete with horns, to fit over his head. He could see through the eye sockets, but no one could see any of his facial features. A goat skin cape complete with hair covered his neck and shoulders and the upper part of his back and chest. Leggings made from goat hide and hair covered his legs from just above the knees down to the floor. The same type of goatskin covered his arms from just above his elbows, down over his wrists and hands. Other than the goatskins, Xanateo was totally naked. He definitely looked like he was half-goat and half-man. It certainly had the desired effect on Sara that he wanted, as it also had on many inductees before Sara. The terror Sara experienced at the sight of the sexually aroused beast would have caused her to pass out if not for the stimulating drugs she had been forced to consume.

Sara started to scream as he approached her and roared like the demonic monster from hell that he represented. He reached out with both hands and grabbing the beautiful white dress at the neck line and he ripped it completely off with one violent pull. Sara was trying to pull away from the Witches, but to no avail. She repeatedly jerked her arms to free them, but the grip of the Witches was practiced and firm. Sara stood naked before this monster while fear and terror shook the foundations of her being. The Witches then dragged her, and laid her on her back on top of the altar. The witches proceeded to hold Sara down before this creature from hell. Sara begged, cried, and screamed, but none of the Witches paid any attention. All screaming and begging just served to excite the Warlock even more. As the sharp edges of the altar dug into the tender skin of Sara's shoulders, back, and hips, Xanateo, with his knees and hands protected by the goatskin coverings, climbed onto the altar.

As the Witches steadfastly held Sara in position, the Warlock violently forced himself on the young virgin with great purpose. Sara's screams echoed off the walls of the cave-room, but anyone who could have heard her would not have cared. Her pain was so very intense. The drugs she had in her system did not deaden the pain but instead had just the opposite effect. The drugs amplified the pain to an almost unbearable level. The Warlock was oblivious to her screams for the drugs, and his perverse desires had driven him into an absolute sexual frenzy. Sara was violated repeatedly until finally Xanateo climbed off of Sara and stood back at the foot of the altar. As he stood, he reared his head back and screamed the eerie war cry of a demonic conqueror, then stared at the young girl that he had just so brutally violated. Bleeding on the altar, Sara felt such intense pain that she could not comprehend what was happening to her. The Witches concocted another potion of drugs, and Sara was forced again to drink the devilish mixture.

A few moments later she was again held down on the altar. This time she was placed face down. As the women held her down by her arms and legs, the rough sharp edges of the altar dug into her breasts, stomach and thighs. Xanateo climbed back on the altar, and began brutalizing her again; sodomizing her over and over with even more violence than before. The demons residing in Xanateo drove him on and on, and those demons were also relishing in seeing the pain and degradation of the girl. Sara screamed from the pain of the rape and sodomizing until she lost her voice, and then she whimpered and begged in a hoarse gasping whisper for this to please stop. She began to vomit and continued to whimper as she pleaded for them to let her go home. The only result the begging had was to stir the demons even more and to drive the Warlock deeper into his drug crazed frenzy. The more she whimpered, begged and cried, the more force and violence Xanateo used in the attack.

Finally, after nearly an hour-and-a-half, he stood at the foot of the altar, staring at the raped and sodomized child. He reared his head and began to speak toward the low ceiling of the cave-room. He chanted over and over: "This virgin is given to you, Somne Octe, this innocence is destroyed as a sacrifice to you, Somne Octe, and this virgin's blood is a sacrifice to you, O Great One."

Over and over he chanted as he pronounced the destruction of Sara's world as she had known it. Somne Octe watched with great pleasure at the evil being perpetrated in his honor. The young girl, a child, was being violated in the most perverse ways, by the half-man half-animal. The shame was complete, the pain complete, the degradation complete. Yes, this one, after she is completely broken, will be a great addition to the faithful. The sacrifice was completed according to doctrine and instruction, but Somne Octe desired that Sara should have more shame and pain before he would be satiated, and he instructed Xanateo of such.

When Xanateo was finished with the girl, he told the Witches they could have her for one week. He instructed that they could do anything they wanted with her, or to her, without scarring, deforming, or killing her. He would return in seven days to begin her training. The Witches looked at each other with such knowing evil that even the gates of hell were most likely shuddering. The demons that possessed each of the Witches were ecstatic with anticipation of the coming week, and what they would cause to be done to this child. Sara was whimpering, crying, begging, bleeding, and throwing up as they led her off to the other part of the Witches' Coven house. They would rest for a while, clean the girl up, and then.....

It was sunrise, April 19.

Chapter 3

That same morning on an oil and gas field in the brush country of South Texas:

The breaking light of the rising sun glistened off the dewdrops on the scrub brush growing on this harsh landscape. One hundred and ten thousand acres of nearly worthless land comprised this ranch, with grass so scarce that it would take well over a hundred acres to support one cow. Ranching had all but ceased when the first gas wells were drilled. A few cattle, less than a hundred, still wandered over the low rolling hills that were covered with scrub mesquite trees and a multitude of thorny bushes. This was hard land, with precious little water, sometimes no water. This was a lonely land. The only person on this nearly two hundred square miles was the lone employee working for the company that held the oil and gas lease on the land. With two hundred square miles, less than a hundred cows, one man, and thorns growing everywhere, this absolutely was a harsh, desolate, and extremely lonely land. It was a good place for this employee of South Texas Exploration Inc. as he enjoyed the solitude, and this ranch was a place of extreme solitude. Extreme solitude was the order of this day, again.

As the company pick-up truck ground to a stop, James stepped out onto the white gravel-covered ground, stretched his back muscles and prepared to spend another day laboring on the oil lease. He was here to do what he did twenty-eight days out of every month. He was a Field Gauger, and it was a guager's responsibility to keep the natural gas flowing from seventeen thousand feet deep in the ground to the large sub-surface pipelines that carried it to far away cities. James' job was keeping up with the amounts of gas produced, and the by-products of that gas, and keeping it flowing to an energy hungry world. Fourteen workdays, then two days off was the routine. Today was no different than any other day. He had gotten out of bed at four a.m., stopped by the coffee shop, ate an enormous breakfast as usual, and arrived at the ranch just before sun-up. It was a sixty-mile drive on a straight and barren road to get to the ranch, and then the process of going through ten locked gates to deep within the property was the normal morning routine. He brought the pick-up truck to a stop and walked to the first of the many gas wells and tank storage batteries he was to check, record, and regulate that day. There was an improved gravel road to each of the sixteen gas well locations on the ranch, but to record and service some of them, James would stop on the main gravel road and take a short cut, walking through the brush and undergrowth to check the well. The walk gave him some exercise, loosening his muscles from the long hours in the pickup, and helped to break the monotony of the day.

This land had its fair share of varmints: coyotes, bobcats, mountain lions, armadillos, and many others, but the king of all is the brush country rattlesnake. Growing to nine feet in length and with a body as thick as a weight lifter's arm, these true monsters are the nemesis of this harsh land. The danger of these venom carriers is never far from the mind of anyone who ever worked or hunted in this area of Texas. The danger was especially prevalent at this time of the year, when the behemoth sized snakes were coming out of hibernation and migrating to their hunting and breeding areas. This morning, one particular snake lay coiled under a Huajilla bush, a dark-green scrub of a bush that was very thick with smallish leaves and large thorns. It was the perfect ambush spot for this nocturnal hunter. A game trail ran adjacent to the bush and there was a small clearing underneath the bush between the snake and the trail. The snake was very well concealed and lay motionless, coiled and ready to strike. He had lain there all night waiting for a rabbit, a ground squirrel, or some other food source to come down the trail, but as yet nothing had been within range of his deadly strike. With the sun coming up, the snake was on the verge of crawling to a place with more protection from the soon to be scorching sunlight; he would return at dusk to seek a meal.

But then the snake felt a vibration; something was moving near him and he stirred, tightening his muscles, preparing, and readying himself to strike, kill and eat the unsuspecting varmint. This was the point where Mother Nature would make the battle for survival a little fairer. As a rattlesnake tenses its body in preparation for a strike, the rattles at the tail end of its body begin to sound off loudly. The rattles always give a warning to an otherwise unsuspecting quarry, but this snake had no rattlers as they had been lost in one form of accident or another. This is not commonplace but it does happen. The locals call this particular type of snake a "Silent Sam," the most dangerous form of the already dangerous rattlesnake. This particular "Silent Sam" was in instant ready-mode, with its tongue flicking and sensing the air for signs of the quarry.

Snakes do not see as humans do; the eyes are used to pick up heat intensities. Colors ranging from gray to yellow to dark red were what its brain sensed from the eyes. This, along with scents sensed from its flickering forked tongue, and vibrations sensed along its radial side lines, gives the snake all the information it needs to take a quarry for its meal. James was walking down the small game trail, stretching, trying to get the kinks out of his body, readying himself for the day, and overcoming the long commute to work. He was always alert to the dangers of the area, even when his mind was seemingly on the work of the day, but being alert is no protection against a Silent Sam. As James' cowboy boot crunched down on the ground by the Huajilla bush, the snake saw a concentration of bright colors. The reaction was automatic and immediate: the snake's mouth opening wide, the fangs protruding straight out as he lunged forward. The snake struck with the power of a running back at the colors that indicated the most heat closest to the snake, the boot. To the snake the heat source could have been a rabbit or most any other animal, but it was the oil field worker's boot. With a speed that can reach well over a hundred miles per hour, the snake struck burying its venom filled fangs just below the ankle area into the cowboy boot. Immediately the muscles in the snake's head around the venom storage sacs reacted, clamping down and squeezing the venom sacs to pump all available venom into its hapless victim.

The force of the strike drove James' boot, foot, leg, and lower body sideways with great violent force. The left leg that was hit was driven into the right leg, and both feet were knocked completely out from under him. As James came crashing down towards the ground, his immediate thought was that he had been shot in the leg. In the short second before he hit the ground he surmised that he had walked up on smugglers and that they had shot him. These smugglers frequently used this area to bring illegal immigrants and/or drugs to the United States from Mexico. In an impulse reaction, he reached to his rear mounted belt holster with his right hand and drew his customized .45 automatic pistol. He was accustomed to wearing the cut-away holster in the back as this protected the easily drawn gun from being accidentally un-holstered when James was walking through the brush; and the handgun was accessible to either hand.

By the time his body thudded to the ground, James had spun in the air, landing belly down on both elbows with the gun in firing position, pointed in the direction from which he supposed the shot had came. The adrenaline was pumping, masking the pain in his lower leg. The fogginess in his mind from the early morning was gone; his vision was clear and his reactions remained on full alert. Through the dust kicked up by his collision with the ground, James scanned the brush, looking for the tell-tale shape of a smuggler. What he saw was not a smuggler, but a snake. Not just a snake, but a big snake. Not just a big snake, but a really big and really ugly snake. James' mind cranked out thoughts, plans, and options at an extremely rapid rate as he squeezed the trigger and shot the snake in the face. As James was still on high alert and scanning the area for other dangers, he glanced back to the snake that was still flopping and coiling even though it was already dead.

He thought, "This is the ugliest snake I have ever seen in my life... one big, bad, and ugly to the bone snake."

As the adrenaline flow slowed in his system, the throbbing and pulsating pain in his lower leg became nearly overwhelming and jolted him back to the reality of the situation. Positioning his body where he could see his lower leg, a groan emerged from his lips. Sticking out of the boot on his left leg was the butt end of two fangs. James could feel liquid, which he assumed to be blood, on the inside of the boot. His ankle and foot were swelling at an alarming rate. As James processed the available information, the prognosis was not good. With a snake bite and at least sixty miles to the nearest town, and ten locked gates to go through, it would be at least two hours before medical help could be obtained. No, it did not look good. James surmised that the snake had gotten him really well in the ankle area and broken off the fangs in the tough hide of the boot when it had recoiled to strike again. Looking at the end of two fangs sticking out of his boot, James thought it no wonder that snake was so ugly, with broken off fangs and its busted mouth. But there were more serious matters to be taken care of at this juncture than to be concerned about the snake's ugliness.

Rolling his body to lean back against a mesquite tree, James considered the situation and what would be his best approach. His ankle and foot had swollen so fast and so extreme that the boot could not be pulled off to access the snakebite for treatment. Reaching for his belt which carried the folding knife he kept beside the .45 auto's holster, he pulled out the custom, titanium-bladed cutting piece. One of the top custom craftsmen in the United States, J.L. Liles of Arkansas, had made the knife for James. Sharp as any razor blade and strong as a blacksmith's anvil, the knife had served James well over the couple of years he had owned it.

Single handedly flipping open the five-and-a-half inch serrated blade, the wounded man was still assessing his situation. No doubt about it, the boot had to be cut off. The swelling continued and was now so severe that it would be absolutely impossible to do otherwise. The cowboy boots had been hand made of elephant's hide almost two months before at a cost of half a month's pay; destroying one of them was certainly not relished, but it was necessary. The knife sliced through the leather uppers of the boot and continued smoothly downward even through the triple-layered area of the heel support. Cutting out the area around the protruding fangs, James stopped, looked inside the gap, and was totally amazed at what he saw.

The venom-pumping fangs had penetrated the triple-layered area of the boot, passing through the elephant hide's outer layer, the bull hide stiffener, and the soft, calf hide inner layer. The fangs had then penetrated the thick, white athletic sock in the ankle area, and passed back out of the sock and into the base of the boot heel area. Neither the ankle nor the foot had been penetrated, not even scratched. His ankle was bruised, sprained, probably broken, and swelling at an alarming rate, but James was not snake bitten. A large sigh escaped James' lips. A full half-cup of venom was soaking the sock and inside of the boot, but none had made it into James' foot, ankle, or leg. The amount of venom in the boot would have caused major damage such as an amputation, or possibly even death if it had been injected into his leg. In entering the boot, the fangs had curved down and missed entering the ankle and the foot. The incident was so close to disaster that two extremely dark purple bruises were appearing and quickly darkening nearly three inches apart where the front upper curve of the fangs slammed into the flesh just short of penetration.

James thought, "What in the hell are the odds of that?"

He struggled to get up off the ground and hobbled, on one leg, the short distance back to the pickup truck. He retrieved the following items from the large tool box in his pickup: a towel, a sack of ice from the ice chest (one of three that he had purchased earlier that morning), and a pint of Jack Daniel's Black Label whiskey that had been purchased the night before. James had placed the Jack Daniel's in the ice chest so it would be ice cold for consumption a little later on that morning. This was a daily event. Another pint, maybe two, would be bought and drank before bedtime along with several (sometimes many) beers used as chasers. The last stop, before going home for the day, was to purchase another pint and more ice to be placed in the ice chest. Then the cycle would be started over the next day. At twenty-seven years old, Jim was big, strong, healthy, smart, and savvy, but with the drinking problem of a much older man. Right now he had a bigger problem to worry about – caring for the ankle and foot that the big, ugly snake had severely damaged.

Hobbling back to, sitting down on the ground, leaning back against the mesquite tree; and propping the swelling and discolored ankle and foot on a low bush; he then fashioned an ice pack with the towel. He applied the ice pack by tying it on the lower part of his leg and around his foot, with strips he cut from the towel with his knife. James leaned back, took a deep breath, and reflected on what had occurred so early in the day and the prospects for the rest of the day. Applying the ice and keeping his foot propped up would handle the swelling and the whiskey would handle the pain, he just had to be patient. He opened the bottle of Jack Daniel's, took a long drink, and from habit swished the burning liquid around in his mouth before swallowing. This ritual was repeated in about three minutes, then again a short time later. James was staring at the dead snake as he reached for the bottle the fourth time, when things changed again. Out of the corner of his eye, he saw someone standing beside the tree to his right.

"Oh my God!" he thought, "I have let a smuggler, a coyote, sneak up on me. Here I am with a broken ankle and foot, about to be shot and robbed or getting my truck stolen, and I've been sitting here staring at that ugly snake."

Relying on past combat and survival training, James ignored the pain in his left leg and quickly spun around on the ground. At the same time he retrieved his pistol, for the second time this morning, except this time he used his left hand because the danger was to his right. He was fully intent on shooting this intruder, whoever it was. His mind quickly told him that he had the advantage because the now fully risen sun was at his back. He would have a clear, sunlit view of the intruder while the intruder would be at least partially blinded by the sun. His mind raced, rationalizing what he was about to do, justifying the shooting of someone he did not even know, convincing himself that the only way to survive was to shoot first.

These drug smugglers, "coyotes," as they are often called, were the scum of the earth. They preyed on those they were supposedly helping, promising the illegal immigrants that they were being smuggled to the United States for a chance at a better life, but when problems arose they would take the women and any valuables they could steal from the men. They would abandon the men to die of thirst, lost in an inhospitable and unknown land, and the women and children would be raped or sold into sex slavery or sweat shops if they lasted that long. James had helped many a poor immigrant with food and water that had been abandoned by the "coyotes." If these coyotes were not ferrying human cargo, then they would be bringing in drugs to be sold on the streets to the children of America. These scavengers would kill you and steal your vehicle without remorse. Today James planned on surviving because he was going to shoot first. His finger was already squeezing the two-pound pull trigger even before his vision was fully focused on the target and his sight picture complete. He was less than one-tenth of a second from sending two hundred and forty grains of copper coated lead into the intruder when he received the greatest shock of his life!

He was fully expecting to see a dark skinned, five and a half foot tall Mexican in the sight picture of his .45; someone armed to the teeth, probably mustached, and wearing a straw hat. What he saw stopped him in his tracks and the pressure being applied by the trigger finger was slackened and then removed. He completely forgot the pain, the snake, the thoughts of smugglers, and the desperate situation of the day. The .45 automatic was slowly lowered, now hanging down towards the ground at the end of a slack left arm. James wasn't fearful at what he saw, but 'surprised' or 'taken aback' would not describe how he felt either. Pain or no pain, ugly snake or no ugly snake, whiskey or no whiskey, this rebellious, hard-drinking young man was about to meet his destiny in a way he never imagined.

Standing by the mesquite tree was a large man; well, a man of sorts, and seemed to be somewhere between seven and eight feet tall. James realized that what he was looking at was something so far out of the ordinary that his mind was having problems processing the situation. The being that was standing there appeared stoic, with bright, white clothes or a coat, light colored if not glowing skin, and a stern but kind face. James felt as though he knew this person, but he also knew that he did not know him. He felt at ease but at the same time he didn't. He slowly came to the realization that this being meant no harm.

The being raised his hand and spoke, "Peace, I am here to bring good news from the Lord."

With his mind really going into overload, James reluctantly and slowly came to realize that what he was confronted with was an Angel, a messenger from God. He had heard and read about this, but here it was, in the flesh so to speak.

His next thought was that he had nearly shot the Angel. "Oh my God! I pulled a gun on a real, live, honest-to-God Angel; I am in deep crapola now!"

The voice of the messenger was as the appearance of his face, kind and firm at the same time. Over the next few moments, James was told that it was imperative that he answer the call of his life and to do it now. The Angel went on to say that he and other Angels had been protecting him from self-destruction and death for thirteen years, and that protection had been to keep James safe to answer the call. There was also the implication that the protection was about to end without compliance on James' part.

James was further instructed that a part of this calling that had not previously revealed to him was "to go to a barren place and bring deliverance from captivity one that was bound."

The Angel talked about other things that had happened in the past, and things that would take place in the future. The Angel stood there for a good while as James tried with much difficulty to absorb what was happening, and then the messenger was gone as quickly as he had came. After James had calmed himself as much as possible, he struggled to his feet – actually, foot – and hopped over to where the Angel had been standing. He noticed a set of large footprints in the powdery dust, with no tracks coming to or leaving the spot, just two prints side by side in the dust. It did not take a lot of snap to figure out that something exceptionally dramatic had occurred, and James knew without a doubt that he had arrived at the crossroads of his life.

He cautiously sat back down by the tree, propped his foot up to tie on the ice pack which had fallen off in the commotion, and tried to assimilate the events of the past few moments. He knew that he had seen an Angel. He knew that Angels were sent from God to do things such as deliver messages. He fully understood what the messenger was referring to about a calling on his life. He wished he didn't know, but he did. James wanted to run and hide, but he had been doing that for far too many years. He wanted to deny what had happened, but how could he do that? He leaned his head back against the trunk of the mesquite tree, reached for and retrieved the half empty pint of bourbon, took off the cap, and looked at the nerve-calming, memory-erasing, pain-killing liquid. He stared at the bottle for a long moment or two while in deep concentration, and then poured the rest of the Jack Daniel's Black Label out on the ground. As he watched the amber liquid soak into the parched ground, he let his memory overtake his thought patterns. It had been a long time since he had not tried to control every thought that might enter his mind, to not remember anything of the past and forget those things that he did not want to deal with. He had been trying to convince himself for years that if someone didn't think about something, then maybe it did not really exist.

Chapter 4

Fifteen years earlier, in Corpus Christi, Texas.

The full-scale Pentecostal/Charismatic church service was nearing a fever pitch at the small Pentecostal Holiness Church in the coastal town of Corpus Christi, Texas. The worship service had started a little before 11:00 a.m. on a hot and humid Sunday morning. Of course, it was always hot and humid in August in south Texas. The music played for over an hour and then the preaching had lasted for nearly two hours more. Then more music and praying had continued for another hour. It was now after 3 p.m. and there were no signs that the service would come to an end. Some people were prostrate on the floor, having been 'slain in the Spirit,' passing out. Others were shouting loudly and dancing around and around, totally immersed in the mood of the moment. A couple of elderly ladies were running at full speed, circling the room with their "Sunday go to meeting dresses" hiked up to their knees and their knee-high, flesh colored stockings held up by big, round rubber bands. They had been doing this for over an hour and showed no sign of tiring. They were shouting something, but no one seemed to know or care what they were shouting. People surrounded the prayer altar, crying, praying, and speaking in tongues and/or hollering out in various ways.

Others sat quietly and worshipped; nearly everyone was worshipping God in their own way. A few non-believers just sat and observed the commotion. It was very hot and the slow-moving ceiling fans did little to relieve the stifling, moisture-laden air. Many held hand fans with the name of a local funeral parlor printed on them. They fanned themselves with the beat of the music, but it did little to relieve the heat. The musicians were in a spiritual hypnotic trance and played on and on and on, well beyond any normal human ability to do so. The music was repetitive and the instruments varied, with drums, electric guitars, piano, accordion, fiddle and others. The music was not the normal funeral dirge style that was found in the major denominational Churches. This was upbeat music with a fast tempo, a mix of country and "rock and roll" (a new craze that had swept the nation a few years earlier). It was the gospel rock-a-billy that had invaded the churches on the outside of the mainstream, the churches that were "across the tracks," and the music was very loud.

James sat in the front row and listened to the music, letting the emotions of the service flood into his being. At his home church in River Bend there had been some exuberant services, but nothing like this. James had become a believer in Jesus Christ at an early age, getting on his knees at the prayer rail and begging God to forgive him for all the dastardly deeds that he had committed by the age of eight. He was dutifully baptized and had tried to follow the teachings of the Bible, as well as he was able to understand them. Sometimes it was difficult – not the following, but the understanding. The church did not help much in the instruction of understanding, but it emphasized emotion and excitement, and that kept the boy at nearly every service that had taken place since his experience at the prayer rail. For four years he had shown much interest in the things of the Spirit, going to Sunday school and church services, church summer camps, revivals, and anything else related to the church. He spent much time listening to the sermons on the radio and even taking correspondence lessons, always taking copious amounts of notes and trying to figure it all out, most of the time without much success.

This service was different. The Evangelist had preached on servitude and the power of modern day healing for over two hours and the words were swirling in James' mind. The Evangelist had quoted verse after verse without reading them from his Bible. It was as though the man had the complete Bible in his head. James had never been so enthralled about anything in all his twelve years. As the service grew in intensity and volume, the Evangelist approached the boy in the front row.

He laid both hands on the boy's head and started speaking at the top of his voice. "This one is called, this one is called, Lord God Almighty! This one is called. We have a chosen one in our midst. This one is called, this one is called." The Evangelist shouted this over and over, increasing his volume with every word.

The local Pastor came over and laid his hands on James as well, and began to speak in tongues and shout. As James stood, his knees got weak and he fell to the floor. At least two-dozen members of the congregation ran to him and laid their hands on the young man and started praying and prophesying over him. James would not understand what all took place that day until many years later. After about an hour, James realized where he was and what was going on around him. He was on the floor, praying in tongues, and the other Believers were praying, shouting, prophesying, and laying hands on him. The Evangelist told him to go to the pulpit and speak the "Word of God," and that he had the calling to preach, the calling to heal, and the calling to cast out demons. He was instructed to go to the pulpit and ask if anyone needed to be healed, then to invoke the name of Jesus and heal anyone who responded. He was instructed not to think about it, just to believe what the Word of God said and to do what the Word said to do.

As James stood in front of the fifty or sixty souls that were gathered that day, his stomach was doing flip-flops. His voice had already changed as he had entered puberty at the age of nine, but he just knew his voice was going to squeak. It didn't.

The boy did not know what he was going to say but he opened his mouth and started speaking. "The Word of God says you must repent of your sins and believe. If you believe in your heart and confess with your mouth, you will be saved. My Jesus is on the throne, and the Word says that by His stripes we are healed. I believe it, do you?"

He repeated it several times. After what seemed like forever, a very large woman, probably in her mid-fifties, struggled out of her pew, walked to the front, and stood before James. Somehow the boy knew in his heart what the problem was when she first started to come forward. Now that she was close, it was confirmed; a large goiter hung on the side of her neck. It was nearly the size of the large woman's meaty fist.

The boy repeated, "My Jesus is on the throne, and the Word says that by His stripes we are healed. I believe it, do you?"

"Yes!"

"Do you?"

"Yes!"

"Do you?"

"Yes!"

"Then be healed in the Name of Jesus to the Glory of God the Father!"

James reached out and gently touched the goiter with his left hand. The woman shot back about ten feet, bounced off the front row pew, and crashed to the floor with a resounding thud! The room became absolutely silent. Everyone was afraid to be the first to move or speak. The electricity in the air was so thick that later some folks said they could hear it crackle.

James spoke, "She is healed; give God the Glory and thanks be to His Son Jesus Christ."

The woman's husband, a small, frail man, eased out of the pew where he had been seated and went over to where the woman was crumpled on the floor. He carefully looked down and then began to loudly shout, "It's gone, it's gone, dear Lord God Almighty, it's gone, it's gone, it's gone!"

Instant pandemonium broke out in that hot, sultry building. Those who knew the woman but were not true Believers accepted the Faith that afternoon and night, and many more were miraculously healed or set free from various ailments and evil spirits. James prayed for some and the Evangelist prayed for others. The calling was to preach and teach the Word of God to a lost and dying world. The calling was to bring salvation, healing, and deliverance to all who would hear.

James knew about the calling, but had tried to forget it, to run from it. He knew what the Angel was referring to when he had said that now was the time to answer the call.

For nearly two years after the events at the Church in Corpus Christi, James had devoted himself completely to the study of the Bible. Never missing a service and attending a variety of different churches, he prayed for anyone that he could, delivering the Word from any pulpit that was made available to him. He just wanted to learn more and more about the Bible and to tell people about Jesus. He didn't want to be like some of the Evangelists he had seen. He didn't want to wear fancy clothes and talk people out of their money. He just wanted them to feel what he was feeling, to know the love of God and the freedom that God's love brings.

James was just a kid, a big, overgrown, quickly-maturing kid, but a kid all the same. His hormones were on overload and he became more and more confused about what he really wanted and what really mattered. He wanted what he thought was this 'calling', but he also wanted to be a teenager. He just did not see how he could be both. There was a real battle beginning to take place inside of James, with the calling on one side and his hormones on the other. The hormones won out. A little over two years after that frantic and fantastic service where the Evangelist had laid hands on him and prophesied the calling on his life, James walked – no, he ran – from God and from the Faith.

He continued to attend church, but where he attended was dictated by the promiscuity of the girls at that particular church. The growing boy became involved in whatever was necessary to keep his mind off of the Faith. He turned to fighting, sports, sex, hunting, fishing, drinking, and whatever else it took to avoid the calling and the Faith. As James grew older and the call became stronger, he needed more diversions to avoid the constant tugging of the Faith: college, weight-lifting, martial arts, brushes with the law, hate groups, spent over a year in Vietnam, fighting as a mercenary in foreign wars, violence, marriage, a family, drinking, more drinking, and more drinking. He did all of those things and much more to avoid the calling, but the pull was there on a daily basis. He avoided answering the call, but no matter how hard he ran or where he hid, the pull was always there. He had denied it and had tried desperately to avoid the exact message that the Angel brought today. Yes, it had been thirteen years since he had walked and then ran from the Faith, thirteen years of running from something that it was impossible to run from, hiding from something that was impossible to hide from.

As James sat on the ground, waiting for the pain and swelling of the wounded ankle and foot to subside somewhat he considered what had came to pass; old memories knocked on the door of his conscience once again. He knew what the Angel was talking about when he spoke of the calling. He also knew what was being referenced as protecting him from himself and from death. Some of it seemed very long ago, but one incident was not that long in the past.

Chapter 5

Two years earlier in the jungles of Central America.

"Uno, dos, tres, fuego!" commanded the Commandant of the clandestine prison in the jungles of Central America. "One, two, three, fire" was the command, and six U.S. made thirty caliber M-2 carbines fired simultaneously, emptying their twenty round clips of cartridges. The hundred and twenty rounds were fired at three men tied to an adobe wall. The ancient wall of the long forgotten Mayan Temple had been fashioned with steel studs to which ropes were tied, and those ropes held three men to the wall. They were spaced about six feet from each other and two of them were blindfolded. The firing squad stood no more than thirty feet from the men at the wall. That wall was pockmarked from previous executions, and the massive bloodstains, pieces of flesh, and brain matter that covered the wall were thickly covered with flies. The ground was soggy with blood and pieces of flesh and fragmented body parts. Flies and maggots were mingled with the gory mess. This execution spot was a very busy place. At the wall, the one man without a blindfold stared at the men who were preparing to fire the rifles. James thought that this was going to be a sorry ending for what started out to be such an idealistic adventure.

The adventure had started a few months earlier with an ex-marine James had met in a biker bar in the outskirts of Houston, Texas. One thing led to another and three weeks later He was training to go to this backwater country in Central America. James was there to fight in a revolution that was intended to free the masses from the tyranny of a communist government. This started out as an idealistic venture and an opportunity to make a lot of money. It sounded like the real deal to James, especially at that stage of his life. He had been married for a few years and had a child, but he had no real direction in his life. The chance to make a lot of money in a short period of time seemed right to him. Why not free the oppressed, live a great adventure, and get a large chunk of money in the process? After completing the three months of training, James took his family to a small island in the Caribbean, off the coast of Honduras, where he put them up in a small resort, pre-paying for six months. The training money and the advances from the mercenary recruiters had been good, and the completion bonus would be even better.

He spent four months fighting in a war that was for a great and glorious cause, and all went well, up to a point. Living in the jungle, fighting the tyrannical communist oppressors, he found that being a part of the war, the liberation, was actually very exciting. Strange as it might seem, James had really been enjoying fighting in the revolution. The fire fights, living in the jungle, the hero's welcome when a village was liberated from those that had held it captive and abused the inhabitants all had added to the excitement of this adventure. That excitement was short-lived after the revolution was successful. When it should have been a time of celebration for the foreign fighters, the new provisional government arrested all of the mercenaries.

This action of the newly installed government created a lot of confusion. Who were the real leaders? Who was going to run the military? There was a great fear among local revolutionist the hat the mercenaries might try to take over the provisional government. The provisional government was a loosely-fit consortium of groups with differently held political views that had run the revolution, and now that it was over nobody seemed to know what was going on. Power plays were taking place at all levels in the chaos. James wouldn't throw a major fit over the arrest; what else could he do but just wait it out? After all, he was being paid per diem by the recruiters, and he had confidence in those recruiters to fix this situation. They had proven to be very trustworthy so far, and there was no reason to expect them not to continue in that trustworthiness. Every day he was held there was another day on the payroll.

James had been held in the jungle outpost and subjected to various types of minor interrogation and torture for a little over a week when things got decidedly worse. One day, a makeshift military court was convened in the jungle camp. An illiterate Judge sentenced James and all of the other mercenaries at the camp to death for illegal entry and carrying weapons.

James dealt with the situation as he had dealt with most other setbacks in his life, thinking, "if this was the way it is; then this is the way that it is."

His only real concern was what would happen to his pregnant wife and their young son, who were waiting on that small Caribbean island for his return. He wondered if the group that had recruited him would take care of his family as promised if he died in the revolution. He deeply believed that they would keep their word, but he also knew that one never knows. When they tied Jim to the wall for the execution, he refused the blindfold and the cigarette; it was way too late to start smoking now. He stared at those who were about to kill him and the thoughts that ran through his mind were of Jesus on the cross. Strangely, he thought, "Forgive them for they know not what they do." James asked God to forgive him for the many sins that he had committed and readied himself to die. After the instructions to fire, the automatic rifles recoiled as the bullets slammed into the group that was tied to the bloody wall.

James automatically tensed his body and instinctively looked toward heaven. He felt that he still believed in God, but his life had certainly not shown it over the past decade. He knew that he would soon have answers for everything he had always wondered about. He felt no pain. He looked at the other men tied to the wall beside him, one was limp with his head nearly shot off and the other was jerking and screaming as the blood spurted out of the many holes in his body. The guards laughed and laughed and then took James back to the lock-up. For nine days straight he was taken from his cell, tied to the wall, offered a blindfold and a smoke, both of which he refused, and then he watched men die. Every day they would untie him, laugh at and taunt him, and return him to the holding cell.

Every day the guards taunted James in their broken English, by telling him, "Today you die, today gringo, today you die." But James did not die.

The jeep drove into the camp on a Thursday and the Officer in the passenger seat ordered that the mercenaries be brought out of the lock up. The officer seemed totally shocked that James and two others were the only ones left. James was permitted to shower and shave, issued new clothes, and then stood up in front of the Officer. A Medal of Valor was hung around James' neck, he was taken to a makeshift airfield, placed on an old DC3 from the 1930s, given travel money, and told never to speak of these events nor return to the country. James was eventually flown to the Caribbean island of Roatan and united with his family. He had found out that his prison camp was the only one in which any of the prisoners had been executed. Emotionally and physically he was a wreck but after a few days with his family on the beautiful island he was well on the road to recovery. The recruiting group had kept their word and James received a relatively large sum of cash for his service. In just under two months, after recuperating completely, James and his family returned to the States and he continued to run from God and his calling.

Yes, the Angels had protected him from death for thirteen years, on this and many other occasions. There were times in James' life that he had nearly convinced himself that he was invincible, but now he knew the truth. Yes, he finally understood that he was protected; he knew not only why, but also by whom. God was the provider of the protection he had always felt in his life. It was time to reconsider his life, his purpose, his future, and most importantly his Faith. The Angels had protected him from death, both physically and thereby spiritually, and he understood. Truly, he had been protected from all harm do to his calling. As he sat against the tree on that desolate ranch, the tears began to run down his face. He began to pray to the God that he had always known was there, but tried to hide from. Sorrow, shame, and then repentance, full and real, filled his very being. He cried out for forgiveness and committed to fulfill the calling on his life, no matter what it entailed. He thanked God for the protection, for God's mercy, for God's Son, for God's love, for the family God had given him, and finally began to thank God for the calling.

James, with great difficulty, checked the rest of the gas wells and made the arduous drive home. He called in the production report and notified the company of the injuries. He would have nearly six weeks to meditate on the events of today, re-align his thinking, and lay down a road map for the future. After he shared the events that had taken place with his wife, he requested that she and the children go to his parents for a stay. James felt he needed the solitude to fast, pray, hear, and respond. He needed also to seek understanding of the part of the message about a barren place and the deliverance of a captive.

Chapter 6

The mountains of Mexico; seven days after the indoctrination of Sara.

In the Coven House in Lleno, Sara was in a total state of shock. The brutal rape and torturous treatment of the week before had left her with severe physical pain, yet her mental state was far worse. The degradation of the past week, and the time of shame with the Brujas swirled through her brain like a flock of evil blackbirds. No matter how she tried, she could not forget the things that Xanateo and the Witches had forced on her. The hurt, pain, disgust, and humiliation were all that she could think about. She constantly recalled the ordeal with Xanateo and the pain and shame associated with what they had forced her to do. On the rare occasion when her thoughts were not on that event, they were on the many perverse things that had been done by the witches after Xanateo had left. Of course, there was no way she could not constantly dwell on these things, for the demons that resided in her were controlling her thought patterns and they relished in reminding her. Their assignment was to torment and torment they did.

More and more evil spirits had moved into Sara as that week progressed. With each perverse sexual act, a demon that specialized in that particular area would take up residence. With the pain that was to be imposed on her, those demons best suited for operating and controlling by pain moved in. A colony of evilness resided within Sara, headed by her familiar spirit Basar. He was the head of all who had been chosen to inhabit, control, and torture Sara into total and complete submission. These evil ones had done this many times over the years, and they knew exactly what was expected of them and how to best accomplish their evil task. The submission of this girl had to be complete if she was to be trained in the ways of Brujeria. She would also be used for other deeds, and there could be nothing of her former being left to interfere. These well-trained and obedient evil ones work mainly in the battlefield of one's mind, in the thought patterns, but, if necessary, the ones best suited for physical pain would gladly do their duty. This day excited the evil hosts; Xanateo would be returning and Sara would be prepared for the next phase of her training.

Sara was understandably fearful of the return of Xanateo. Based on her previous experience, she could feel nothing except fear. Her trepidation was unfounded as Xanateo didn't have the drive or the desire to deal with her sexually. His perverse and demonically inspired sexual drive had always been to brutalize and rape young virgins. Having an outlet for that perversion was one of the main reasons that he became a Warlock. He could fulfill his perverse and demonic sexual drive and not have any concerns about problems with the "Policia" or other authorities. After all, the real authority in this area of Mexico was his superior one, Somne Octe. At this juncture, Xanateo's only interest was getting the girl grounded, trained, and practiced in the craft of "Tellings" so she could get on with the business of making him money and spreading fear. As for his perversions, there would be another girl very soon and then another and...

The first meeting between the two was short and to the point. Sitting down at the eating table, the Warlock explained to Sara what was expected of her.

"You will do as you are instructed. You will not complain nor disobey my brujas. Whatever they tell you to do, you will do immediately and with a smile on that pretty little face," the Warlock spoke with firmness and determination.

Sara answered in the manner the witches had instructed her, "Yes, Master Xanateo, as you say."

Xanateo laughed and responded, "I see you have already been learning well from my other servants. Obedience is necessary and absolute. If you do not obey, here is what will happen to you..."

The Warlock waved his hand as a signal to the evil host residing in Sara. A burning pain began in her groin and spread up her young body. It was as though she was on fire, burning from the inside out. There was also a severe jabbing pain in her groin area that reminded her of the rape and brutalization of the week before. The pain and the burning increased in intensity until she didn't think she could stand it any longer. Screaming and falling to the floor, she thrashed around and pulled at her groin area, trying to remove something that wasn't there. The pain was so intense, she sought the solace of passing out, but it was not permitted. Her mind filled with horrid images of her family being burned alive and especially of her younger sisters. She could see them as clear as if they were standing in the room. and it was as though the flesh was melting off their faces. They were looking at Sara, screaming for her to please stop it, stop the pain.

This extreme torment continued for about fifteen minutes, then the pain in her groin subsided and her mind cleared.

"See, my little pretty one, it will always be best to obey completely," Xanateo said ever so quietly and sincerely.

Sara nodded and knew that trying to endure that type of torture would be futile. She knew then and there that she would have to be as cooperative as she could. She consoled herself with the idea that the witches seemed very satisfied and happy, and maybe, just maybe, some day she would be happy.

The training began and continued for six months. As long as she was obedient, learned what was taught, and practiced for hours on end, life was bearable. The bruja Josefa was assigned to be her overseer and instructor. Josefa was the most learned of the group in the ways of Brujeria. Though not the eldest, she had been entrusted with the ancient books and writings that had been handed down for hundreds of years, some of them for thousands of years. She liked Sara and decided to teach her of the ways of the "Old Ones." Josefa was the only one in the Coven that was literate and when she realized that Sara could read fairly well, especially for her age, Josefa became very excited.

The training started with the elements of allowing the familiar spirit, Balzar, to speak through her in the séances and prophecy sessions. All she had to do was to let him speak, but there was a lot of showmanship that went along with it in order to extract the greatest amount of payment from those villagers she was servicing. It all had to be convincing to the "Customers" that she was the one responsible for the revelations. Learning how to sprinkle the ground with magnesium and to place copper powder mixed with gunpowder on the candles was an art in itself. The flash had to appear impromptu and utterly amaze the customer with the dazzle of multi-colors and sounds, but it wasn't meant to frighten them to the point of running away. Presentation was everything and it was grilled into her over and over until she had perfected the task. Timing was another integral part of the process. To know when to go from one part of the presentation to the next and knowing exactly when to start the prophecy was paramount, but knowing when to ask for more money and gifts was the ultimate goal. The importance of this had nothing to do with Balzar, but rather with extracting the maximum amount of payment from the recipient. The goal was to amaze and impress those who came with a lot of pomp and flash, let the demon do his thing, then get all the payment possible, and then some. They wanted to fully convince those paying that it was the girl, the flash, and the pomp that brought the prophecies, not an evil spirit. Most people would pay dearly for someone to be able to speak of their past and project their future. Also, most people would run if they knew they were dealing directly with the dark side, with evil spirits and demons. Sara was doing very well in the training, receiving only a few disciplinarian attacks from the evil ones.

The times the girl enjoyed most were late at night, when Josefa would take out the ancient manuscripts. After retrieving them from their hiding place and very carefully unwrapping them, she show them to Sara. All were written in foreign languages, with many of them in cuneiform. The trainee was extremely impressed by the strange writings and symbols in these manuscripts; some were written on papyrus, some on leather, and some on pieces of thin, flat stone. Josefa could not read the symbols at first, but her familiar spirit had interpreted them for her until she could. The bruja and the trainee spent many hours on many evenings looking at the manuscripts and drawing the many symbols in the dirt floor of their hut. Sara had no idea what was meant by the symbols but when she followed the instructions of Josefa and drew them in the dirt there was a stirring deep inside her, similar to the excitement of the night of the last bath. Neither the instructor nor the instructed knew exactly what one of the seemingly most powerful manuscripts represented, but they were told it was a copy of an ancient spell and incantation manual that far out dated even the Egyptian Book of the Dead.

This was the guidebook for ancient magicians and those serving Satan thousands of years in the past, the book of which there were not supposed to be any existing copies. Sara watched, as Josefa would do the spells and incantations with the accompanying manifestations. Sara had heard about, but had never been to, the movie theaters with a giant moving picture on a wall for people to watch. Sometimes the manifestations of the spells and incantations were moving pictures of strange looking people building giant pyramids, preparing their dead, or even at battle. The images were in the center of the room instead of on the wall. Sara could walk around them and look at them from all angles. At other times, a spirit would come and tell them things in response to the symbols being drawn and the incantations spoken. The spirit never appeared as evil or frightening, but as an elderly "maestro" (teacher). This was all very exciting to the young girl from the mountains. Yes, there was much to learn, and as exciting as all the spiritual things were, most of her time was still spent practicing the art of fortune telling.

Reading facial expressions, eyes, and body language took some time to fully resonate with Sara. The client who had come for some knowledge of the future or for guidance in some area had to be worked for the best effect, and to extract the most payment.

"Look into their eyes, Sara, look into their eyes," instructed Josefa with a knowing smile on her lips.

"What am I looking for?" asked the student.

"You are looking for surprise and fear – fear, not terror," Josefa went on. "Look for surprise when you do the flashes and the incantations. Look for fear when you tell them a secret about themselves. If you don't see this, then do or say something bolder and bolder until you do. If you see terror in their eyes, you must back off until the terror reduces to fear," the bruja was leaning very close to Sara now and almost whispering. "Terror will cause them to flee and we will not make much money. Then it will be our turn to have real terror and real pain from Xanateo and the demons," she stated quietly, not as a matter of intimidation, but as a matter of fact."

With excitement in her eyes, Sara told Josefa, "Yes, I can and will do that." She was becoming both excited and anxious about all that was happening.

The girl was instructed to watch how the person was sitting and how they held their arms, and to especially watch their jaws. The instructions were of course totally foreign to her, but she learned. If they are sitting back in their chair, then you don't have their attention. If they are leaning forward and intently staring at your mouth, it is time to ask for some money. If they have their arms folded, you must do something quickly or else you will lose them altogether. If they have their jaw jutting forward, shock them with some of the flash and permit your spirit guide to mention a past event that the client felt had been a secret. If their jaw is slack and their mouth slightly open, ask for more money and seek for your spirit-guide to speak. If all seems to be going well, then she was to lean forward and then back, and if anyone else did the same, ask for more money. On and on went the instructions: if they do this or that, then you respond with this or that. It confused Sara at first, but she was bright and caught on quickly.

At the end of the six months, Josefa had a serious talk with her protégé. Sara was told that the life she would live for the next eighteen months would be the proving ground for her future as a bruja. She was told that as long as she did as instructed, there would be no problems. If she disobeyed or if she did not bring in the required amount of money, the punishment would be brutal. Sara had experienced the torture of the evil ones that lived inside her and she related this to Josefa. Josefa responded that that was bad enough but that if she did not get sufficient money from the 'tellings', as they are called, the punishment would be far worse than she had experienced in the past. "Sufficient money" could best be described as all the valuables that the person had or could get. If Sara could not accomplish this, then she would be rented out as a sex slave to bring in more money. Josefa explained that this had happened to her many times before she became so old as not to have value in that area.

"Sara," Josefa spoke almost with kindness in her voice, "the torture and pain that you went through on that first night is nothing compared to what you will suffer at the hands of those men who pay Xanateo for young girls." Her voice stiffened as she said, "Do what you are told, bring in the money, don't develop any feelings for those who come to pay and listen to you, and you will not suffer more than you will be able to bear."

Sara considered this and thought that it would not be a problem. She just had to watch their eyes and do as instructed. Sara did not know it at the time, but the fear in the eyes of some of those who would be across the table from her would be her downfall.

Chapter 7

Six months after Sara's training started, in the small desert village of San Bastian.

The village was over sixty miles from the nearest paved road, isolated, barren, and filled with almost destitute people. The poverty and the hardness of this area are almost impossible to describe. Water was so scarce that drinking water had to be gathered from scraping the early morning dew off of the few leaf bearing plants that scarcely populate the area. Extracting the liquid from the inside of the numerous barrel cacti that dotted the almost barren landscape also provided water. The liquid that was produced in these plants from the dew was sour and bitter tasting but it did prevent dehydration. A few patches of black beans and some small fields of parched corn were all that could be grown, and the failure rate of those agricultural endeavors was astronomical. Poorly nourished goats and a few chickens provided nutritional support for these destitute desert dwellers. The goat's milk was turned into cheese and this combined with the sparse amount of black beans, corn, cactus pears, various roots, and meat from the few wild animals that were hunted were the staples. The main non-domesticated animal used for food was the desert rat, a rodent that seemingly could survive anywhere. On occasion, a rattlesnake would be killed and it was treated as a delicacy. One could look at this place and wonder why anyone would choose to live here. The answer is simple, it was their land, and land ownership meant more to the people in these villages than anything else.

They had lived on this land for hundreds of years serving the rich land owners, but it had been "Their" land since the revolution in 1915 led by Pancho Villa and his band; they would weather drought, hunger, heat, and anything else to be able to say, "Mi tierra!" (My land!).

San Bastian seemed a poor choice for the brujas to ply their trade. But beneath the poverty striken exterior and among the truly impoverished was a group of extremely evil and wealthy individuals. These were the "banditos" (bandits). For generations their families had robbed individuals as they traveled through the desert on their way from one city to another in Mexico. What the land lacked in productivity it more than made up for with potential victims. When better roads were built and tourism became popular after World War II, they would rob the Americans and Canadians traveling to exotic places such as Mexico City, Acapulco, or Central America. Without exception when someone wanted to travel south of the United States by vehicle, they had to travel down the "Highway of the Americas." That well-traveled road was just sixty miles from San Bastian. The banditos considered this to be their destiny, their inherited right to rob those traveling through this land. Travel advisories in the United States had warned about this area for decades. The advisories had warned travelers not to stop along this stretch of highway for any reason, as the bandits would fake automobile accidents, sickness, or whatever to aid in their thievery. One of the most common ploys was for the thieves to dress as policemen and stop tourists at an official looking roadblock. The tourist would be relieved of money and other valuables, usually without major harm coming to them or their vehicle. The exception was when resistance was offered, and the bandits would deal severely with the resisters. Beatings, rape and being stranded on foot would result from the slightest resistance. Highway bandits were and still are a problem, but the more violent individuals had found a new source of income. They were now "contrabandistas" (smugglers) of the most brutal sort.

High in the Andes Mountains of South America, a bitter tasting leaf from a small tree had to be hand picked by the descendents of the ancient Inca Indians. The leaves were then transported to the remote high mountainous jungle areas of Columbia and processed in crude laboratories. The process was a simple one: break down the leaves by cooking them and purify the core substance using ether, alcohol and other chemicals. The result was nearly one hundred percent pure cocaine, and the demand for that cocaine was reaching epidemic proportions in the United States and Canada.

The purified cocaine powder was bundled and transported to the northern coast of Colombia. There it was loaded onto boats of all sizes and shapes. The boats would travel north across the Caribbean and into the Gulf of Mexico. The final destination of the armada of drug bearing vessels would be one of the eastern Mexican port cities: Chetumal, Vera Cruz, or Tampico, with Vera Cruz being the offloading port of choice. The Port of Vera Cruz is the world's leading exporter of a wide variety of fruits and vegetables. At any one time there are hundreds of small freighters and large cargo ships from all over the world coming and going. This constant produce and fruit carrying traffic makes it almost impossible to track the cocaine carrying vessels mixed among them. The "white gold" (cocaine) is then loaded onto large double-trailered trucks, some boxcar tractor-trailers, some tankers, and some that resembled produce or fruit transporters. The trucks then travel up and over the eastern mountain range to the central highlands and head north across the vast desert area. At the north side of the desert, in and around the larger northern Mexican cities of Monterrey and Montehuala, the heavy loads of "white gold" on the trucks are broken down into lighter loads and loaded on smaller vehicles. The smaller vehicles are then sent from that reloading location to various border towns in Texas, New Mexico, Arizona, and California. The cocaine is then broken down into even smaller loads and loaded into vehicles to cross the border or stashed in the back-packs of individuals who then swim the Rio Grande River, or hike across the dry desert border of the western states.. Some of the product is loaded onto small planes and flown below radar detection towards to the north. This is the track of most of the illegal drugs that enter the United States. Flying loads direct from Columbia was tried at the beginning of the drug epidemic, but the loss rate made it an inefficient means for the drug cartels. The "white gold" highway through Mexico quickly became the route of choice.

The first part of the journey from Vera Cruz over the mountains to the south end of the desert is a protected and guaranteed safe journey. This protection is paid for by the bribery of government officials. The last part of the journey through Mexico, from the northern part of the desert, the reloading spots, all the way to the border, is protected in the same manner. Protection in the desert area presented a problem to Columbian cartel plans. The desert area, which includes San Bastian, is classified as a "no man's land." The Federal or the State policing agencies just do not go into the area. The whole area is filled with bandits who would rather shoot an authority figure than look at one. The Columbians struck deals with the more violent and organized bandit groups, and it seemed to be a deal made in hell, so to speak. The "banditos" were now called "contrabandistas" (Smugglers) and would run shotgun (protection) for the heavy-laden trucks across the hundreds of miles of desert. They would place one to three vehicles of heavily armed men to the front of the trucks and spread out over one to five miles, and do the same to the rear of the trucks. They had sophisticated communication equipment, the latest in armament including RPGs (rocket propelled grenade), and were not just ready for a fight; they relished even the thought of one. The rare times when other smuggling groups, regular bandits, or a law enforcement group would attempt to interfere, the bandits used extreme violence and many deaths would occur. Of course, none of these confrontations or deaths were ever reported or investigated. The contrabandistas, for their service, were paid all the cocaine they wanted for their personal use, as well as very large sums of American dollars.

The lifestyle of drug smugglers that is generally accepted, the fancy houses, cars, planes, and all the rest, does not apply here. The cash was stacked in one or another of the adobe dwellings in San Bastian. The cocaine was consumed constantly and in almost fatal amounts. Fancy cars or homes held no great concern for these brutal smugglers. They were into violence: violence in their work, violence in sex, violence with their families, and violence with anyone that they had contact. They ruled everything with fear and enforced that rule with more fear and violence. The demons, which influenced them and sometimes totally controlled them, knew no bounds in regards to the violence. No one ever bothered their stacks of cash, their stores of arms, their vehicles, or even their dogs. When it was necessary for someone to walk past the area of town that they occupied, the intruders' heads were kept bowed and the eyes never even glanced in the direction of their dwellings. To do otherwise would bring a beating, gang rape, or even death. There was only one thing that these thugs were more dedicated to than their violence and that was the religion practiced by the group. They were all dedicated to a fanatical and most extreme ancient religion called Santeria.

Santeria finds its roots in ancient Babylonian Empire; from there it moved into ancient Egypt. Migrating through Africa after the fall of the Egyptian Empire, it soon became the religion of choice of the northern and central portions of that continent. When the slaves were brought from those areas of Africa to the Western hemisphere, the religion that came with them then became perversely intermingled with Catholicism. The salves, in an attempt not to upset their masters, renamed the demon lords that they worshipped and sought to appease. The new names were the names of accepted and notable saints of the Catholic Church, hence the name Santeria (Way of The Saints). Thus, the practitioners of this black art could speak freely and not upset their owners or the Church. Santeria and its various diluted forms are practiced in most western hemisphere countries, with approximately five hundred thousand adherents in the United States alone.

The typical Santera ceremony in the United States is held on a Saturday and most of the adherents are immigrants from Cuba, Haiti, and Africa. Everyone arrives early, dressed in their patron Saints, their Orisha's (Demons that are passed off as Catholic Saints) favorite colors. With them they bring bundles and boxes containing the sacrificial animals, special foods, and offerings needed for the ceremony. The ceremonies are long and exhausting. They can last a few hours, or all night and into Sunday morning.

A large room of the house will be used and especially prepared for the ceremony. The time passes with conversation and nervous jokes. The altar is placed in a prominent position within the ceremonial area. Commonly, images of Christ and the Catholic Saints are prominently displayed to facilitate the fallacy of the religion as Christian. Spread out before each image is a large ceramic cauldron with a cover, usually decorated in a very brightly painted style. These cauldrons contain the stones, sacred to the ruling demons, and the consecrated seashells used in the ceremony. Upon the mat covering the floor before the altar, the participants place the fruits, vegetables, cooked foods and the sacrificial animals they brought to the ceremony. There are also containers of "Chequete" (a drink made from sour orange juice, molasses, corn meal and fresh coconut milk). Bottles of "aguardiente" (an extremely strong alcoholic drink, distilled from sugar cane juice) are also placed on the mat as an offering to the demons. The official conducting the ceremony, either a high ranking Bishop or a Priest or Priestess (Santero or Santera) will fill his or her mouth with the "aguardiente" and spray it over those gathered as a blessing and to quiet those who have already been possessed by an "Orisha" prior to the ceremony.

The conversation ceases at a signal from the Santero. Everyone settles down in front of the altar. The Santero holds up a container of "Omiero," a mixture of rain water, river water, sea water, holy water, "aguardiente," honey, corojo butter extracted from the hard nuts of the corojo palm, cocoa butter, powdered eggshell, pepper, and various other herbs and ingredients particular to the mixture's purpose. It is brewed by immersing a live coal wrapped in a fresh banana leaf into the mixture, which has been steeping since the previous day.

The container is presented to the four cardinal points and a small offering is made to each point by spilling a bit of the "Omiero." The Santero faces the altar and offers the "Omiero" to the "Orishas" (demons)sking them to bestow their "Ashe" (magical powers) upon him. A small amount of "Omiero" is then spilled at the room's entrance. The Santero returns to the center of the gathering and spills "Omiero" on the floor three times. The mixture is then offered to all to drink. Usually everyone does. The Santero then draws the required symbols on the floor to summon the demons. They are drawn with powdered eggshell mixed with earth from the roots of the favorite tree or plant of the house's ruling demon. The symbols are blessed and sprinkled with corn meal. A candle is lit at prescribed locations. No one is permitted to walk on these designs or even to step over them.

The preliminaries being over, the youngest initiates (young in terms of time since their initiations into Santeria), along with those that desire to join the group, walk into the room backwards, facing away from the altar. They show submission by laying face down on the floor with their heads towards their godmother or godfather, the person sponsoring the novice and who may or may not be conducting the ceremony. This person, or persons, in turn salutes the demons and blesses the new initiates and the novices. The blessings made, the godfather or godmother stands. The drumming begins.

Sometimes a participant is immediately possessed by a demon. At the moment of possession, the personality traits of the controlling demon become clearly manifested. Shaking and shuddering of the whole body are followed by very strong convulsions. The possessed individual falls on the floor. As the physical symptoms cease, utter calm is reflected in the initiates face. Then the voice, mannerisms and gestures of the one being

R.C. James

possessed change completely. The personality of the one being possessed ceases to exist. The personality of the demon has completely taken over the body of the one being possessed. The possessed one is called "caballo" (horse), best described as one being ridden and under control by the possessing demon.

Nearby persons try to restore the "caballo's" calm by blowing into his or her ears and mouth. Cocoa butter or other ointments are rubbed on the person's hands and feet. If the trance becomes too violent, the "caballo" may be injured. It is the responsibility of those around the possessed individual to ensure that these injuries are not too severe or even fatal. After the initial crisis is over, the demon's control over the possessed body becomes stronger. The demon dances to the welcoming beat of his specific rhythm and chants and "cleans" (purifies and blesses) those present. If the ceremony includes an animal sacrifice, the demon blesses those present by tearing or biting off the heads of sacrificial birds and sprinkling those present with the blood.

If the demon is in a good mood, his "children" (those initiated to that particular demon) will joke and dance with him. If the demon is in a bad mood or comes to punish someone, there is a profound silence. Everyone respectfully listens to the scolding. The demons speak briefly and get directly to the point. They speak directly through the "caballo" or through a cowrie shell or coconut shell held to the ear of one of the onlookers. The trance may last for seconds or for the entire ceremony. The trance ends spontaneously, although the godmother or godfather of the possessed person may have to intervene at times and prevent the possession from lasting too long. This is especially true in the case of novices whose trance capacity is not well known. Rarely can the possessed person remember what they did or said.

‖ 85

The preceding is indicative of a standard, watered-down ceremony as practiced in the United States and most "civilized" areas of the world. The group in San Bastian practiced the original, unaltered version of this form of Satan worship.

Chapter 8

The ceremonies in San Bastian were decidedly different and would sometimes last for days or even as long as a week. The length of a ceremony was determined by the Santera when they were sure the Demons had been appeased. A ceremony was held whenever the Santera came to the village. The bruja Santiaga was their Santera or priestess. Xanateo had schooled her in the art of Santeria and she was respected for her expertise. Xanateo knew it would take much more than just "tellings" to have the power over these violent thugs. They already had many violent demons controlling them and Santeria was the only way to control them and extract much money in the process. He would always send a "teller," a keeper, and Santiaga to this God-forsaken place in the desert. This was to be Sara's first real "telling," not practice, but the real thing. Josefa would keep close watch over her and instruct as needed. Sara and Josefa would be working for offerings of bags of corn or beans and the occasional copper coin, while Santiaga would bring in major cash and drugs for her effort. At a first glance it would seem that the small amount the people had to give Sara and Josefa was not worth the effort, but all the villagers had to respect Xanateo's Coven.

A group of "contrabandistas" gathered for the Santeria service in one of the adobe huts on the backside of the small, desolate town. Each of them brought large amounts of American dollars and cocaine to please the demons and as payment to the 'Santera' Santiaga. They also brought strong rum, cigars, and other items to appease each of their chosen, and soon to be summoned, demons. The leader of the group, Ramon, also had a most foreboding looking black leather bag. Santiaga had prepared the room in advance with mats to sit on, positioned in a circle on the floor, symbols drawn on the floor in a white powder made from seashells, and a large cooking pot set in the middle of the room. A drum made of male goatskin stretched over an open frame of human thigh bones was set to one side. There were also two thigh bones laying on top of the stretched goatskin for use as drumsticks. Many lit candles had also been placed around the ceremonial hut. On a small table that Santiaga would use were an assortment of utensils, powders, liquids and many others items to conduct the service. The only sounds made during the arrival of the nine men were the squawking of the chickens and the squealing of the pig that had been brought to offer as sacrifices to the evil ones. Each of the nine took a place at the circle and set their bags in front of them. The chickens and the pig were then tied in feed bags and stacked against the wall.

Author's note: The rest of this chapter may be too graphic for some readers. If you are sensitive to graphic details about the baseness of man, and the inhumane treatment of animals and each other, please skip to next chapter. This may be done without detriment to the flow of the story.

Santiaga had put on a full-length, bright-orange robe and a large amulet hanging from a gold chain around her neck. The ceremony began with all of them chanting in unison. Over and over the men chanted phrases that had no meaning to them. They knew the power of the "Santera" and did as she instructed. Santiaga started the lengthy process of appeasing the evil spirits or "gods" and "saints", as they were called in this hellish atmosphere. She poured purified water and the other required liquids into the cooking pot, then started the wood fire beneath the cauldron. She asked each one present what they had brought as an offering.

Each of the hardened individuals emptied the sacks they had brought with them into the pot. A favorite piece of jewelry or any other thing that carried meaning to the individual was tossed into the large pot. All eyes were on Ramon as he opened the leather bag and pulled out of it a backbone of a recently deceased human corpse. It was so fresh that decay had not set in, so fresh that the meat clinging to the bone was still reddish in color. Ramon had raided a nearby cemetery the night before and retrieved the backbone of a man who had been buried two days before that. As the cauldron began to boil on the wood fire, the chanting resumed and became louder and louder. The participants drank some of the hellish mixture from the cauldron and Santiaga continued the art of her black magic.

The men believed that if they pleased the "gods" that protection would be given for their drug-running ventures. If they all became "Caballos" then they would have favor on the next illicit outing. One of the younger men was the first to become possessed. He began to foam at the mouth and was instructed to start making rhythm on the goatskin drum. In a demon-possessed, hypnotic trance, he picked up the human thigh bones and began to beat out a rhythm. The possessing demons controlled him and chose the rhythm as he pounded it out and would continue to due so until the ceremony was over. Next, the "Santera" beheaded the chickens and the squirting blood from their necks was sprayed onto each of the men. The ceremony then turned to utter chaos and decadence. The men readily drank of the chicken blood and the mixture from the cauldron as each became fully possessed.

The pig was then tied to a stake that was driven in the ground next to the boiling pot of gifts and human remains. The Santera reached under the animal and deftly slit its stomach open with a ceremonial knife. With its entrails spilling out on the dirt floor and then being stomped on and torn apart by the wild gyrations of the animal itself, the pig slowly and agonizingly died of blood loss. As the drumbeat went on and on, the pig was making an enormous amount of noise during its death gyrations. The men were all wallowing in the mire on the floor, and the demons were more than pleased. This continued into the night until the demons were satiated and released the humans. The last act of the evening was Santiaga demanding the ultimate offering to fully appease the "gods" and guarantee the protection needed for the group. She told the leader of the group, Ramon, that they had brought the wrong number of men to the ceremony.

"The number nine is not pleasing to the gods," she screamed at Ramon. "Earth, wind, fire, water, north, east, south, west, north, east, south, west, earth, wind, fire, water, eight signs, eight worshippers, not nine, the number is eight. The gods demand the number be brought to eight!"

Ramon did not hesitate as he grabbed a young man that was next to him by the neck and held him on the ground. The others joined in holding the man down in the mire as Ramon took a machete and started chopping at the young man who was actually Ramon's own Nephew. Ramon began to hack the backbone out of the young man's body while he was still alive. The young man suffered greatly, but after a time his suffering stopped as the machete severed the spinal cord at the base of the neck. The gory mess of the backbone was thrown in the boiling cauldron to be ingested by the group. The group had well pleased the "gods" and protection would be theirs. Somne Octe and his hoards that had been watching the carnage were very pleased. Santiaga left that night with two kilos of nearly pure cocaine and over thirty thousand American dollars in crisp new hundred-dollar bills.

At the other end of the village, Sara was not making that kind of money, but for her first "telling" it was going satisfactory. She enjoyed toying with the men that had lined up to hear what she had to say about their lives. She felt very powerful when the men across the table from her started showing fear in their eyes. She recalled how to act and react and when to ask her familiar spirit to speak. Josefa looked on like a proud parent as Sara did just exactly as she had been instructed. After all the men had been dealt with, the women began to come in.

A young woman told Sara that she needed to have a baby soon or else her husband would abandon her and take another woman. Sara knew that her assignment was to get all the valuables possible from the situation. She knew that she had to tell the young woman to go and bring all the valuables that she and her family had. When the valuables were in the possession of the Coven, Sara would perform the "magic" that would permit the woman to become pregnant. The young woman, whose name was Camila, reminded Sara of her sisters back in San Mateo. She knew the customs of the men in the area: your wife has children, mostly boys, or you get rid of her. She felt compassion for this woman and her situation. Fear came into Camila's eyes when Sara told her to bring a large amount of valuables and then the wish would be granted. The woman stated that she had nothing of value. Basar began to speak. It was the first time he had done this without Sara asking him. Basar spoke through Sara and told the girl that without the required payment she would never become pregnant.

The booming voice of Basar said, "Go to the contrabandistas and sell your body to them and bring the money, or you will be shamed and rejected by your husband and your family."

As fear turned into terror on Camila's face, Sara's heart began to melt for her. Sara tried to resist Basar's speaking but the effort was to no avail. The sympathetic feeling in his host sent various terrible feelings through Basar and the other resident evil spirits. He responded immediately by instructing one of the underling evil spirits residing in Sara to go to Xanateo. Xanateo was fifty miles away setting up the next weeks "tellings." After informing the Warlock of the impending disaster, the evil spirit was told to return and to watch Sara closely, and if her weakness persisted to have Josefa take her place.

"I will be in San Bastian tomorrow afternoon and if the situation persists, I will deal with her then." Xanateo almost spit the words out of his mouth.

He knew that if just once sympathy was shown by one of his charges that the news would spread like wildfire and his reputation would be badly damaged. This could not and would not happen. The demons in Sara started their tormenting and she fell to the floor and screamed as the burning pain started in her groin and soon became unbearable. The young woman, Camila, tried to run but was restrained by Josefa.

Josefa told her, "This is your fault, go and do what you must and bring the money here tonight."

Camila began to protest, "I have never been with anyone except my husband, and I could not do as you are asking."

The reply was quick, "If you don't, you will not have a husband, and besides, it is not something that you don't do every day with your husband. Go and bring the money."

Camila looked at Sara on the floor, thought about the evilness of the contrabandistas, and considered the shame and hurt of being rejected by a husband. She sighed deeply and walked slowly out the door. Some of the other women came for a "telling," and each was like a repeat of the situation with the young woman, Camila. All Sara could think about was her mother and her sisters, and she could not drive these clients to the edge of terror. Josefa was watching this with great fear in her own heart, knowing what would happen to Sara if she did not cease this childishness. Josefa had spent six months training this young one, and Xanateo would also have some of her hide. She would not have to endure what Sara was going to endure but Xanateo would certainly turn the demons loose to punish her for improper training. She kept trying, pleading even with Sara to just do what she had been trained to do.

"You don't know these people, we will be gone tomorrow, just do what I have told you to do," she pleaded.

Sara was starting to get more and more confused about the conflicting feelings inside her, and Josefa took over the "telling." The rest of the night went on with Josefa working the remaining women, and Sara sitting in a corner of the room. She continued to suffer reoccurring pains in her groin and the terrible images of her family. When the last of the villagers had been serviced, Josefa and Sara made their way to the camp and rested. The rest would be needed.

Josefa spoke quietly, with sincerity in her voice, "I am sorry for what is going to happen to you tomorrow. I know, for it happened to me many times. You must, you must get control of your emotions. You must!"

The next day came without further incident, but when Xanateo arrived at the village, things changed. He gathered the group and immediately released the demons to punish Josefa. She screamed in pain and fell to the floor, rolling over and clutching her stomach area. Blood began to trickle out of her mouth and then spewed from her with each scream.

The Warlock turned to Sara and said, "See what you have caused, see the pain you bring to the one who has cared for you and instructed you."

Sara, with terror in her eyes replied, "Stop it, stop it, I will do whatever you say, please stop it."

Xanateo did not acknowledge her but turned to Santiaga and instructed her to dress Sara in little girl's clothes. She must be made to look even younger that she really was. After this was done and while Josefa was still on the floor in pain, the demons were released on Sara. The burning and stabbing pain in her groin and the vision of her mother and sisters overwhelmed her. After approximately minutes the attack stopped and Sara was approached by the witch and instructed to accompany the Warlock.

"You will do as you are told," He stated, "every time you resist even in the smallest way the pain will return, and with each return it will get worse."

Xanateo and Sara walked across the village toward the dwellings owned by the "contrabandistas." On the way, the demons were released to bring Sara pain a number of times. They stopped at the place where Ramon lived. Xanateo told Ramon that he had a gift for him as a reward for his faithfulness. As Ramon looked at Sara, her appearance was that of an eight or nine-year-old. His perverse desires were overwhelming and almost uncontrollable as he stared at the child. Spittle ran down his chin and his breathing became much labored. Ramon was told that she was a virgin and he could have her overnight and until noon the next day. With the perverse drives rising inside of him, he would not notice that he had just been lied to, nor would he care.

"Do as you will with her, just do not kill her or scar her too badly." With that statement, Xanateo could hardly contain his pleasure in what was about to befall this little disobedient one.
As Xanateo walked back through the village, he took a different route. He wanted all the villagers to see him and to be struck with the fear that the Warlock was walking through their village. As he neared the center of San Bastian, in one of the compounds with two small mud huts, there was a tremendous amount of turmoil. The women were wailing, screaming, and crying uncontrollably. Xanateo dismissed them as just being another miserably weak link of the human race. If he had taken a closer look he would have seen the family of Camila, the young woman who came the night before seeking aid to get pregnant. Their wailing and crying was for Camila who had been found dead early in the morning. The pain and shame she felt for her situation was more than she could bear. She could not sell her body, nor could she face her husband. She had taken a knife from the kitchen hut and went out behind the animal pens to cut her wrists. She had sat on the ground holding a crucifix that became covered with

her blood as she died. The evil spirits had been rejoicing as the young woman could not face her future and decided to end it. It had been another victorious night for the dark forces of evil whose goal is to kill, steal, and destroy.

Late the next morning, Josefa went to retrieve Sara. The girl could hardly walk from the violent abuses of the night before. True to instructions, she was not dead or scarred, at least not on the outside. The corruption and perversion she had been subjected to by the men the night before would forever be in the shadows of her mind. After a week, Sara was able to go back to doing the "tellings." She was much more inclined to do as instructed, but periodically her sympathy and empathy for the younger women would bring on the attacks, the pain, the terrible images, and more nights of abuse.

Chapter 9

May 5, two years after the initiation of Sara, in San Rafael, a small town in the high desert of Mexico.

The teenage girl sat on the edge of the dry gully and looked out at the setting sun. Although this day, Cinco de Mayo, is the 'Fourth of July' of Mexico, there would be no celebrating for Sara tonight. It would not be long before she would be about her duties for the night, and she was trying, without much success, to forget the horror of the events that had taken place in her life. One long day turned into another long day and then into another. It had been two years since the witches and Xanateo had come for her in the village. The sexual abuse from Xanateo that first night had not been repeated, but for the last eighteen months there had been times when many strangers raped her. The routine was the same: when she would exhibit kindness towards those who came for a "telling," the demonic host inside would torture her and then she'd be sexually abused by strangers. She did not see Josefa much during this time, only on rare occasions, and these rare occasions were the only bright spots in her life of darkness.

After the fiasco in San Bastian, she had been passed around from witch to witch, continuing her work as a 'teller of the future' and learning the art of witchcraft. Sara had become frail, sickly and miserable. Sunset seemed to be the only time of the day when she was not tormented both physically and mentally by the host of evil spirits that resided in her. The pain, the torture, the vicious attacks, and the relentlessness of the internal abuse were seemingly constant, with the rare exception. Her mind at this particular time was not being overtaken by bodily pain and/or mental torment, and was surprisingly clear. She looked across the gully, noticing a few scraggily goats grazing on the sparse vegetation. She remembered a far better time, when she herded goats on many occasions in the beautiful mountains around her home village of San Mateo. She watched the young goats prancing and jumping with no concern for anything except the moment. She had been like that once, playing, teasing with her siblings, running and laughing, but it seemed so long ago. A small smile started at the corner of her mouth as she reflected on those pleasant events. She even giggled out loud as she thought about one especially fun day when her brother had slipped and rolled down the mountain. He had been so cocky about his climbing skills and there he was rolling unceremoniously down the side of Jefe Mountain. It was so funny, he was so embarrassed, Sara and her sisters laughed and laughed and laughed.

The pain hit Sara like a bullet passing through her body. She cried out and grabbed her lower abdomen and groin, doubling over to the ground. The demons, which had been resting, would not allow this one to be joyous. She had not learned the complete obedience that she must have to keep her feelings in line with the wishes of the demon and the control that would keep the punishment away from her. It was the demons' duty to bring misery and pain, to destroy and steal, to kill, and to keep Sara under the constant pressure of oppression. Their assignment was to use fear, pain, and humiliation to bring her under total submission. If Somne Octe happened to find the girl giggling joyously, it would be a bad day for them in the Principality. There would literally be hell to pay. As Sara sat down in pain, her mind filled with horrid thoughts. Some of the demons within her were specialists in tormenting the mind, and they were very good at what they did. Sara's mind was again immediately filled with thoughts of her parents' home being burned and her sisters on fire. They were trying to escape the growing flames, but the door was blocked, closed by large stones that had been piled against it. Her sisters were screaming, and the flesh was melting from their faces.

Sara grabbed her face and started screaming, "No, no, no, no!" as the vision became more realistic and extremely intense.

This went on for about a half hour, then stillness: no pain, no vision, just stillness. Sara lay without moving, trying not to think, as she knew the demons would resume their attack at the slightest provocation. Sara heard one of the Witches approaching; it was Santiaga and the time had come for her nightly ritual.

She spoke to Sara and said, "Will you ever learn to keep your mind on the things the spirits want, and not on your childishness?"

It was time to go to work doing the "tellings," permitting the demons to speak through her and bring fear to the people and money to the Coven. The anguish and pain brought to the people through her revelations and the extortion and the abuses never seemed to end.

Sara had not proved in the last eighteen months of training to be a good candidate for a witch. She had too much of a soft heart, even after months of torture and abuse; it seemed she would never, on her own, be able to perform the duties required. She cared too much about the people, and had difficulty keeping in line with the destructive duties appointed to her. They would have killed her, but she looked so young and innocent that a plan for her still existed. For now she would earn as much money as possible, as the money that was used to further their purposes was a necessity. There was also the possibility that she would change after a longer time of abuse and shame. Xanateo had ordered the witches to use her as long as they fancied and if she didn't learn and submit, to turn her over completely to the demons. He told them that there was a purpose, but it was not to kill her. Santiaga told Sara to change into her séance clothes as it was time to go to work for the night.

Sara begged to be left alone for a while longer. Immediately the pain started in Sara's groin area and grew more and more intense as the young girl cried out, grabbed herself, and felt she could not even dare to breathe. It was as though she was on fire. The visions of her sisters burning and the flesh melting from their faces again filled her mind and she screamed and screamed. After the attack had passed, Sara reluctantly walked to the hut to change. Santiaga looked at her and again asked if she was ever going to learn to be obedient and avoid the attacks.

The night was like so many others, as they took money and jewelry from people in exchange for revealing the past and bringing fear about the future. There was the occasional customer that Sara had a hard time dealing with, and it was usually a younger woman or a teenager. She knew that she would pay for these feelings, but just did not seem to be able to keep them at bay. As events unfolded, this would be another night that Sara would be rented out for the ever-present, perverse sexual desire of demonically controlled individuals in the towns and villages they visited.

This of course was further punishment for her reluctance to keep her feelings out of the "tellings."

The four Ramirez brothers were in town. They were drug growers from a place in the mountains called La Union del Refugio. They both grew and delivered marijuana to the loading points at the south end of the desert. That was where the marijuana was loaded and joined the convoy of "white gold" trucks on the way north to the United States. They struck a financial deal with Santiaga to have Sara for a couple of days. Their goal was to aid their brother by giving him a woman to have sex with. The gift was for their "Little" brother, Pancho, a giant of a man, severely retarded, who had never been with a woman. The Ramirez brothers had watched and encouraged their little brother to be more and more brutal throughout the two days Sara was abused by the giant. The attacks so tore her that it would take over seventy stitches (from the self-taught doctor in the town to her genital area and her anus) to keep her from bleeding to death. Poncho had so severely bitten her lips, ears, breasts, and other parts that the 'doctor' had also much stitching and clamping to do there also.

While she was recovering from her injuries, she would be relegated to working as a maid/slave for the various witches who were taking care of her. Though the freedom from the thought of future forced prostitution was a welcomed relief, the ongoing degradation of her situation was nearly unbearable. Sara deemed it best to just cooperate and try to be like the rest of them. She had decided to become a willing student in the ways of Brujeria. To Sara it seemed as though she had been in this coven forever and that it would never end, but it had only been two years. Sara did not know it, but this phase of her life would soon be over, and her life would become even worse. Sara was now fourteen years old, owned by the warlock and his coven, and the residence of over two hundred evil demonic spirits.

Chapter 10

That same night in Brownsville, Texas.

Although Brownsville is in the United States, you could not tell as the "Cinco de Mayo" celebration took place with even more fervor than in Mexico. The banners, flags, and decorations were all in red, green, and white (the national colors of Mexico). All the signs were in Spanish, and "Norteno Mexican" music blasted into the street from every storefront, car radio, and the various "cajuntas" (bands).

James had resigned from his job in the oil and gas fields and moved to this part of Texas to study and prepare for his calling. He had started a small business to support his family and studies, and life seemed good. He thought many times that all those years of running from the "calling" had really been wasted. He worked, enjoyed his family, went to church, did street ministry, and was the chaplain at the county jail. James preached whenever and wherever he had an opportunity and he felt very content with this life.

Being Chaplain at the jail was a real adventure. This was not just a county jail; it was a Federal holding facility for the Federal Courts located in Brownsville, Texas. It was a large facility full of Federal, State and local doers of evil. There were

Mexican and Columbian drug smugglers, Middle Eastern arms merchants, and a variety of very base criminals from all over the world incarcerated there. The Federal courts were backlogged and sometimes these world-traveling evil-doers were held for as long as two years waiting for trial. In actuality, some of the delay was due to backlog, but most of it was delaying tactics used by highly paid defense lawyers. The longer the trial could be put off, the lower the chance of conviction. This tactic caused severe overcrowding and these lawyers were filing suits to get the criminals released because of the overcrowding. Of course if and when these rich international criminals were, as the jailhouse saying goes, "released on bond, then they were gone."

Not all of the inmates were of the high dollar variety. Intermingled with the foreign inmates were the local, run of the mill lowlifes. Thieves, murderers, rapists, drunks, child support dodgers, wife beaters, drug addicts, child molesters, etc. were the other faces of criminality held there. James spent much time trying to help all to accept Jesus Christ, repent their old ways, and start anew in life. There were some glorious successes and there were many more heart wrenching failures. James readily dealt with all of those that he could, but dealing with the child molesters was exceedingly difficult for him. When he considered the evilness of their perversion, the innocence destroyed in their victims, and their consistency in remaining in their perversion, it took all his faith to even visit with them. In the nearly two years of serving as Chaplain in the jail, at least some of nearly every stripe of criminal incarcerated there came to the saving grace of Jesus Christ, and truly changed their lives. Every type of criminal except the child molesters and the pedophiles who remained in their sin, not even once did James see a pedophile truly repent and accept Christ as Lord and Savior.

This was a place that really tested the faith of any minister. James' wife, Phyllis, ministered to the women's side of the facility and the couple and their growing children seemed well settled. On the outside they seemed settled, but deep within their souls they felt a yearning, a tugging, that constantly pulled at them. It seemed as though there was something else that they should be doing or were going to be doing. They had been raising their family and James had been studying New Testament doctrine and ancient religions. This seemed to be an odd combination but he was sure this was the course to be taken. He was completely sold on the doctrine of Jesus Christ as laid out in the New Testament, but he also had a deep, sincere drive to study the ancient religions. He concentrated on the ancient beliefs and religious customs of the Babylonians and the ancient Egyptians. Neither he nor his wife could ever understand the reason, but the drive was there, and it seemed to satisfy a drive from within them.

That "Cinco de Mayo" night, a Saturday, James attended the men's prayer meeting being held in town. The same evening, Phyllis went to a ladies meeting in the country outside of town. As the events of that night unfolded, James and his family would come face to face with destiny, and their lives would never be the same. During the four-hour prayer meeting, the Spirit of God showed up in a mighty fashion. Some of the men were praying, some shouting, and some in quiet meditation, and James was one of those in quiet meditation. He sat on the floor and waited for the Lord.

The Spirit of God spoke to his spirit and said: "Prepare yourself to be a minister for me in San Mateo, Mexico. You will go and be part of the battle for the hearts and souls of the people of that area."

James was not sure he had heard it right. He did not have a clue as to the location or even the existence of San Mateo, and he certainly had no desire to go and live in Mexico.

As he sat and contemplated what he had heard in his spirit, another man came to him and stated, "James, I feel the Lord would have me to say to you that you are supposed to go to Mexico to a place called San Mateo."

At hearing this, a knot started to grow in James' stomach, and he knew that his life was in another transition.

And yet another one of the attendees said, "Brother I don't know what this means, but the Spirit spoke to me concerning you about freeing someone who is being held captive."

It was brought to James' remembrance what the Angel had said about this same thing in the oil field two years before. "Dear Lord," he thought, "It is all going to come to pass."

Almost as an afterthought one man spoke and said, "I don't have a clue as to what this has to do with anything, but the word I have for you is this, the place is in the middle of the circle."

James groaned in his spirit and thought, "this is all I need right now. A riddle is really all I need right now… 'The place is in the middle of the circle'."

The prayer meeting continued for a while until the men said their goodbyes and left. As James drove home, his mind was filled with thoughts and confusion. What did all this mean? Was it just a coincidence? Were the men good intentioned but just over excited with the praise and prayer of the evening? Was he to go to Mexico to do his ministry? Maybe he was just trying too hard to do the right thing. James argued with himself all the way home. Surely he was not supposed to travel to a foreign land, uproot his family, give up his business, the Chaplain position, his home church, his studies, his friends, and go to some place he had never heard of before tonight, a place that might even not exist; surely not.

James arrived home well before his wife did that evening. He dutifully recorded all that had taken place in the journal that he had started the day of the Angel visitation two years before. Now it was not surprising for the women's prayer meeting to be considerably longer than the men's meeting. He had picked up the children at the church care center, brought them home, bedded them down and waited for Phyllis. While he waited he continued to try and dismiss what had taken place earlier. It was surely one of those times when people just get carried away with the heat of the moment. He knew that when morning came, the stirrings inside him would be just a memory. When Phyllis arrived, her excitement was all over her. She could barely talk as she started to try and relate what took place at the women's meeting.

She stated, "God gave us direction tonight and it was confirmed by three of the other ladies at the meeting."

James stopped her and requested that she please write down exactly what had transpired as he had already done in the journal. After she had written what had taken place at the women's meeting, they sat on the floor and each put their respective recollection of the night's events on the coffee table. They were acting like two kids on Christmas morning. They read each other's papers and both broke into tears and praises unto God. Phyllis and James had written the same things. The calling, the place, the duties and even the spot in the center of the circle were exactly the same. They prayed and praised God until nearly sun-up. Needless to say, the stirrings that James had felt were not just memories that next morning, those stirrings were a desire boiling inside both James and his wife. James duly noted the occurrences of the night before in his journal. They were ecstatic about what God was doing and would spend the next few years in longing expectation of the things to come. It was a long span of years but, as they learned, God's timing is not our timing. They continued working the business, doing ministry at the jail, being active in the church, raising a family, studying the Word of God and ancient religions, and preaching at every place that availed itself. They were very content and daily they grew more anxious at the same time.

Chapter 11

After the Cinco de Mayo incident, Sara healed for two months and then Xanateo's Coven held a meeting in the town of Tula to talk with Sara about her future. The scars left on her face by the attack would not bode well for future "tellings," so they relayed a new plan for Sara. They wanted her to go back to the village of San Mateo, back to her family. She was to blend back into the local populace and not to mention anything that had taken place. She would be elevated to the position of bruja at a later time that would become evident. As they laid out the plan for her she willingly accepted it. She would do anything to get out of the lifestyle that she had been living for over two years.

In San Mateo since Sara had left the village, some of the villagers had become Believers in Jesus Christ – Christians. There were only seven of them, but that was seven too many to suit Somne Octe. The plan concocted by Somne Octe and related to Xanateo was for Sara to return to San Mateo and blend into the community. She was to tell the villagers she had been working for a relative in one of the larger cities. Since this was not an uncommon practice there would be no problems with the story. She was to work at being accepted by the Christians and then, through her, the Christians would be discredited. At point Sara was to be told that she would then be elevated to area bruja. What the Coven told Sara was true, up to a point. They had a plan to discredit the Christians and Sara would definitely be part of it, but she would not become the promised bruja, she would be used in a way that she could never have imagined.

As Sara arrived on the mountain, she was relatively healthy and clean, wearing new clothes and carrying a bag with more clothes. This was a rarity as almost every one in the mountains barley had one change of clothes, much less a variety. Inside of one of the bags was a beautiful, white-lace dress bought for her to wear after she had been accepted by the Christians, for her baptism. Sara moved into the small thatch hut with her sisters and was well received by all, including the small cluster of Christians. The lie was spun about her working as a house cleaner in the city of Victoria with a cousin on her mother's side, and all the villagers believed it. She also spoke of a terrible accident that caused the now fading scars on her face. Sara's parents never mentioned or talked with her about what had transpired in the two years since she had left. Her father never even spoke to her, being full of hate and rage for what had transpired on the "Night of the Spirits."

A month passed and Sara began to visit with those who had become Christians. She played her part well, listening and agreeing with everything told to her. About six weeks later, an Evangelist came to visit, and Sara falsely confessed that she was a believer and wanted to be baptized into the faith. There was much joy among the Christians. Up until then, the members of only one family believed; now, this was the beginning of the expansion of Believers that the Evangelist had been promising. There was a baptism planned for the end of the next week at a creek in a larger town that was about a half-day's travel away. The town was out of the mountains and on a major highway that traversed the area. There were a larger number of Christians in the towns that were dotted along the highway. Churches were also being established in these towns, as it was easy for the American Missionaries to drive to them. For the most part, these Americans ignored the mountainous areas because of the difficulty of travel. The amount of resistance by the locals, who were fearful of witches, was also a factor. The people there were basically receptive to listening to the gospel, but at the same time they felt fearful of the demonic retaliation that would follow if they listened too intently.

This baptism service would draw a few from the mountains and more, maybe hundreds, from up and down the major highway. That day would also be the sixteenth of September, a holiday celebrating another one of the many revolutions of Mexico. Approximately four hundred had gathered for the event, most from the larger towns, some as far as a hundred miles away. They were all singing, rejoicing, visiting, laughing, and praising God. It was a joyful day of fellowship with a "compana" (dinner on the grounds and a service) planned for afterwards. This transpired just exactly as Somne Octe had expected. He relished the dishonor that was about to be brought on these stupid humans, these imbeciles who had chosen not to accept his lord, Lucifer, as the Supreme One.

Thirty-two souls had been baptized before Sara entered the water. She had on the beautiful white dress that Xanateo and his Coven had purchased. The dress has been gathered around her calves and tied with a scarf to keep it from floating up as she entered the water. All around her, hundreds of people were singing and shouting. She dearly loved all the attention she was getting, and she thought of the attention she would receive when she became the bruja of San Mateo. She walked out to the Evangelist with much contempt in her heart for him. How could he be so stupid as to baptize a bruja? As the musicians played and the onlookers sang at the top of their lungs, Sara was positioned to be immersed.

"In the Name of the Father, the Son, and the Holy Ghost I baptize you Sara into the Kingdom of God," said the Evangelist before plunging her below the surface of the water, as he had already done thirty-two times that day.

The demons possessing Sara went into action as they had been commanded by Somne Octe. Sara's body went stiff and floated to the top of the water, her skin turned white, extremely white, and she stopped breathing. Concern swept through the impromptu congregation as they watched what was occurring. The concern soon turned to fear, and then to pandemonium as word scattered through the crowd gathered at the stream that the girl in the white dress had died.

"She's dead, she's dead, the Evangelist has drowned her, she is dead," they screamed as they ran around in circles not knowing what to do or where to go.

Someone with one of the few vehicles rushed into the town to bring a doctor. When the doctor and a police representative arrived, only the seven Christians from San Mateo and the Evangelist were still there with Sara. Everyone else had left, riding, walking, or running anyway. They just wanted to get as far away as they could from this tragedy. They were fearful of an investigation by the authorities, who already had great hatred toward the Christians. They forgot the "Campana" planned to take place after the baptism service. They forgot about the food and fellowship with the other Believers that always followed these services. They forgot everything except that the Evangelist had drowned, killed, this young girl, and they wanted to leave before the authorities or even the Army might come to interrogate them.

Somne Octe heard of this and was more than pleased. "That will show these pathetically weak and stupid humans," he said to no one in particular.

Then he turned to Balzar, one of his senior fallen angel underlings, and said, "Just wait until tonight, there will be no more of these so-called Believers left in our mountains."

The plan that had been concocted before Sara had been informed that she was to go back to San Mateo was now in full implementation. She had been lied to about becoming a witch; she just didn't have the hardness of heart that it took. She showed too many signs of a tender spot in her being, and that was more than enough to get her rejected. Tonight she would be completely turned over to the demons residing in her to bring havoc on those whose fear of the evil ones was starting to wane. When they were through using her to discredit the Christians, the demons would totally destroy the girl. Somne Octe felt great pleasure in knowing that Sara would be tortured beyond what any human could ever imagine, and then her misery would really begin. He gave further instructions to his hoards and departed for another area of the sector he controlled.

The doctor and the police representative got out of the truck and the man that had retrieved them quickly turned the vehicle around and left. Sara lay on her back under a tree by the water's edge. She seemed not to be breathing and her body was cool to the touch. As the doctor kneeled down beside her to do his examination, Sara took a deep breath and sat up. The doctor nearly fainted. The policeman nearly fainted. The Evangelist nearly fainted. And the seven Believers from San Mateo would have run away, except for their responsibility of getting Sara back to San Mateo on Jefe Mountain.

Sara's normal color returned, her body temperature rose to normal, and she asked, demurely, "Where is everybody?"

The doctor and the policeman walked back to the town cursing the crazy Hallelujahs (as the Believers were called) and their crazy ways. The Evangelist went on his way, not understanding any of this. The group from San Mateo, including Sara, caught a ride in an empty cattle truck to the base of the mountain and then walked up the steep trail the few remaining miles to the village. Not one of them had spoken a word since they had left the baptismal creek.

It was well passed dark when the group reached the village; they said nothing to anyone. Sara went to bed shortly after arriving at the family compound. A few hours later, when everyone else in the village was sound asleep, Sara sat straight up in her bed. The pain and the burning in her pelvic area were intensifying quickly. The evilness dwelling in her was instructing her as to what she must do to stop the torture.

She screamed, "No, not again, they promised, no more! I can't do that, please stop, please stop!"

Sara quickly submitted to what the demons were telling her to do. When she tried to argue, the pain would become overbearing and the voices so loud that her ears felt as though they would burst. Sara piled rocks against the door of the sleeping hut of her sisters and the hut her parents were in. She then retrieved corn stalks; the dry ones used for animal feed, and stacked them against the fragile buildings. Every time she tried to stop, the pain and voices overwhelmed her and it was as though she had no will of her own. She went to the cooking shed, stoked the coals, and lit a handful of corn shucks. After she placed the burning shucks on the dry fodder, the fire quickly spread and started consuming the dry sticks of the walls and the thatch roofs of the structures. Sara could see the reoccurring dream come to pass in front of her very eyes. Soon her parents would be dead and the flesh would be melting off the faces of her sisters. She wanted to stop this nightmare, but was unable to do anything except be obedient to what the demons were telling her to do.

A force hit Sara in the stomach with the power of a mule's kick. She fell backwards and doubled over. The pain and burning in her pelvis increased more and more to a level that is indescribable. Sara screamed as loud as possible, but nothing seemed to help. She ripped off her clothes and stood naked in the light of the ever-increasing fire. Great amounts of saliva and then foam began to come out of her mouth and she was so desperately confused that she reached up and started pulling out some of the hair on her head, trying anything that might stop the pain.

That same night, September 16th, nineteen hundred miles to the north, at a motel in Tennessee where he was holding a revival, a horrifying dream woke James. There were people on fire and a young girl was screaming and begging for help. The dream seemed to be taking place in a mountainous area somewhere that he did not recognize. Monsters of many different sorts surrounded the girl and they were clawing and biting her. Other monstrous looking creatures were screaming into the girl's ears. James could clearly see the girl and she seemed to reaching out to him, and to be begging him directly for help. James was visibly shaken as he got out of bed and spent the rest of the night praying and trying to understand what had taken place. He received no solace, just the feeling of a necessity to be prepared. Prepared for what he wondered aloud? He had been traveling for over two weeks, throughout the mid-south, teaching at different Churches and holding seminars. His wife was back in Texas taking care of the business. He had become quite satisfied with his life and this dream was very disturbing. He wondered, "What is this all about? Who is the girl and what am I supposed to do about this?" As the sun came up over the horizon, James was drenched in sweat and shaking noticeably. After he calmed down, he noted the incident in his journal and tried without success to get some rest.

Totally naked, screaming at the top of her voice, foaming at the mouth, and now pulling her hair out by the handful, Sara started running through the village. The animals were raising a major ruckus and some of the villagers were awakened from their sleep. Soon the whole village was awake. They all gathered at the Soto's compound to try to put out the fire. Some of the men broke through the wall on the opposite side of where the fires had been started and the family members were all rescued with just minor burns and sore lungs from the smoke. By the time dawn came, the fires were out and everyone in town was discussing the events. Sara, still screaming and still with the copious amounts of foam coming from her mouth, was running naked around and through the village.

The villagers assumed that Sara was rabid as rabies was not an uncommon thing in such remote areas, and it was her family's responsibility to do whatever must be done to control the girl. An Uncle saddled his horse and chased down the girl, roping her like a calf with a lariat, and then he dragged her behind the horse to the woods up the side of Jefe Mountain away from the village. Without getting off the horse, and not touching the girl, he wound the rope around and around a tree, effectively tying her so she could not run away, move, or hurt anyone. She would be left there for three days and when the Uncle went back, she would either be dead or cured. That was the custom, and had been the custom as long as anyone could remember, when someone was considered to have rabies. Three days later, when the uncle returned, he found the girl was no longer foaming at the mouth, nor was she dead, but she definitely was not cured.

She was screaming over and over, "They are killing me, they are killing me? Why? Why? I did what they wanted!"

She was hog-tied and carried across the back of the horse like a sack of potatoes as the uncle took her back to the family's compound. She was still screaming, still naked, but because of the way she was tied, she could not pull at the remaining hair and did not foam at the mouth. She was placed in a mud brick hut at the family's compound. The hut was used for storing crops when they were gathered and waiting to be used. There were no windows and only one door with no opening in it. It was very damp and dark inside. The stored food was removed; Sara was untied and unceremoniously dumped inside. The family wanted nothing to do with her, but it was the unwritten law of the mountains that they had to deal with it. For two more days the girl screamed, begged, cried and whimpered. Finally the uncle who had chased Sara down, whose name was Carmen Gonzales, came with his wife, Lupita, and told the immediate family that they would take the responsibility of caring for Sara. They would leave her in the hut since it was as strong as any building in the village, and that they would care for her the best they could. A small window was cut in the door and food was thrown in for Sara. A gourd filled with water was pushed through the opening and hung on the inside tied by a string from the outside. If she wanted to eat and drink she could, if she wanted to starve she could.

This situation went unchanged for almost one year. Sara screamed most of the time, being quiet for only brief periods of fifteen or twenty minutes. During that year no one went inside the hut. The closest anyone even got to the hut was when the aunt or uncle would bring food scraps or water to place for the girl. One day Sara was screaming more intensely and louder than usual, and then for the first time in a year she spoke something intelligible.

She began yelling out, "Don't do that, it hurts, leave me alone, you're killing me. Don't do that, stop, stop, stop!"

That same day, September 20th, seven hundred miles to the north, in Brownsville, Texas

James was driving down a dirt road on the way to visit a sick friend. He had a most startling vision. There was a young girl that was apparently standing in the middle of the road; it was so real that he slammed on his brakes to avoid hitting the girl. He recognized her as the one he had the dream about a year before. The same monsters surrounded her, and some of them were wrapping chains around and around her. Other demonic looking creatures were clawing her, and jabbing her with sharp sticks. After he had abruptly stopped, he sat there for a long time, looking at an image that seemed so real he felt as though he could touch it. Slowly the image faded, with the last of it being the girl begging for help and looking directly into James' eyes. Then she turned into what looked like an ice sculpture. His last thought was that he must be ready, and then he wondered where that thought had come from. After a while he composed himself and as he had done for all major, and most minor, events in his life since the Angel, he made a notation in his journal. Then he spent much time in prayer for this unknown girl, and whatever the vision had represented. Much time would pass before James would realize the significance of the vision.

In San Mateo, Sara continued screaming for a short time and then silence. The uncle and aunt waited three days before entering the hut. They were fully expecting to find the girl dead. When they opened the door and their eyes grew accustomed to the darkness, they found her curled up in the fetal position on the filthy floor. To their surprise, she wasn't dead, for upon close inspection she was breathing shallowly. After much discussion, they brought a handmade cot from their compound and made a mattress by weaving a thick grass rope over the frame. They placed Sara directly on the woven grass rope and covered her with a loosely-woven horsehair blanket. The only movement Sara initiated was for her to roll over on her back, stretch out straight, clasp her hands around her own neck, and then stare straight towards the ceiling. The aunt tried to feed her, but to no avail. Sara would not open her mouth. The uncle then retrieved a stick and pried her mouth open, and the aunt forced in some "masa" (soft-ground corn that is used in the making of tortillas. Masa is made from soaking dried corn in lye water to soften the corn into a concoction that resembles mush) and then grinding the mixture with a hand grinder. Masa is the ingredient that corn tortillas are made from. The aunt then held Sara's lips open and pinched her nostrils so she had to open her mouth to breath, and the masa was forced into her mouth. The throat was massaged to force the food down her esophagus. This had worked on sick animals and it seemed to be working well on Sara. Water was forced down her in the same way. Every day the aunt came and forced Sara to ingest masa and water. The days turned into weeks, weeks into months, and month after month after month, the routine was continued.

Another repercussion that came from the events of the baptism day and the ensuing fire was that the Christians in San Mateo were told by the ruling board of the village to cease all Christian external activities. They could meet in the small building they had built or in the family's home, but they could not talk to anyone about their faith. No one could join them except the seven who were already professing belief. They could not carry their Bibles in the open, only to and from the little mud Church, they could not pray in the open, and could not proselytize, period. Any infringement of this and they would be banished from the village. The Christians were blamed for all the turmoil in the village. The leadership of the village believed that the shame, embarrassment, and subsequent danger of the fire was brought on as a result of these Christians, and their beliefs could not be permitted to spread. Somne Octe was so pleased with the events that had taken place that he rewarded Xanateo and his Coven with even more power to wreak havoc on the residents of these mountains.

Chapter 12

Approximately one year after James had the vision on the way to pray for a sick friend in Brownsville, Texas, things had really changed in his and his wife's lives, and were continuing to change. James and his wife had been raised in homes that had held a lot of prejudice toward people from Mexico and some others of this world. When they were children, the general feeling among family and friends alike was one of at least disdain toward the hoards of illegal immigrants that were coming across the border into the states of Texas, New Mexico, Arizona and California. By the time James had become a man, his feelings were not as prejudiced as some others, but might not be considered neutral or reserved. Part of the change that took place in their lives during that period of time was a deep concern James and Phyllis felt for those living in the extreme poverty of most of Mexico and the other countries to the South. It started out in their conversations, then their prayers, and it began to overwhelm James and his wife, eventually this feeling became a driving force that was almost obsessive.

James and Phyllis had started gathering clothing, shoes, food, etc. to send south with every missionary that was going in that direction. James began to read and study the language, culture, and politics of Mexico. What started out as curiosity was soon approaching a compulsion. A deep, heartfelt desire to help those of the Mexican heritage was growing inside of them both. One thing that James began to realize then and to understand over the coming years was the total work of the Holy Spirit. If a person is called by God to go somewhere, then when the time comes to go, the Holy Spirit has that person totally and completely desirous of doing that bidding. It was happening here and would happen many times more in their lives. The support of missionaries and the preparation, study, etc. seemed to the James' to last forever, but change was on the horizon.

Another "God thing" happened to add to the events of the prayer meeting nearly two years before. The winds of change that had started blowing at that prayer meeting were about to become a full-fledged hurricane.

In their early morning-prayer time, on a Saturday morning, the Spirit of God spoke, in an audible voice, telling James and his wife, "It is time to go to Laguna, Mexico. Go first to El Lemon. This is the pathway to San Mateo."

Their obedience to this revelation was sure and quick, with no delays and not much thought about the decision. They were finally going to Mexico and were going to do it as quickly as possible, to seek the places where they had been directed to go. On that same Saturday afternoon, they purchased over one hundred Spanish New Testaments, many witness tracts, and supplies for the trip. On the next evening, at the Sunday night service in their local church, the congregation laid hands on them, praying for their safety and success. James was truly wishing that he knew where El Lemon was located. He now had three names of three locations to go to in Mexico, El Lemon, Laguna, and San Mateo, but he did not know where any of the three were located. James and Phyllis had decided to tell the church only that they were going to Mexico. They did not mention El Lemon, Laguna, or San Mateo. They didn't want to encourage anyone to try to help if it wasn't really a "God thing." As James was praying for guidance for the first part of their venture, a "God thing" happened, and the directions to El Lemon were revealed. This took the breath out of both of them and caused much rejoicing. After hands had been laid on them and a prayer offered, a man that they had never seen before came up to them and said, "If you can, while you are in Mexico, go by a place called El Lemon. It is at the base of the Sierra Madre Oriente Mountains in eastern Mexico. You will be blessed." He also gave them approximate directions.

They crossed the border into Mexico the following morning. They had planned to head south, across the farmlands and then across the deserts of northern Mexico. From the word spoken to them the night before, they had a general idea of where El Lemon was located (within a few hundred miles) and they were so excited. They knew only that they were on a mission for God. They prayed and sang praise songs, and watched the miles roll by.

As the farmland and the desert passed by, the excitement in their spirits grew by leaps and bounds. They watched as the poverty worsened every mile that they went south. The growing compassion in their hearts was nearly overwhelming. They did not have a clue what was going to take place or where it was going to take place, they just knew they could hardly wait. They spent the first night in a motel, if it could be called that, about twelve hours from the border. After eating dinner from the supplies that had been brought with them, and walking around the town for a while, they prayed and discussed the situation. Deciding that trying to make too much of a plan with what little information they had would be futile. From a map purchased in one of the larger cities on the way through Mexico, they ascertained that they were about six hours from where El Lemon was supposed to be. The problem was that there were many El Lemons on the map, so they prayed and asked directions to the correct El Lemon. Plans were made to get up early, eat, and leave by five a.m. They did.

As they approached the region of El Lemon, the terrain changed dramatically. They passed by many orchards: lime, lemon, tangerine, tangelo, orange, grapefruit, and mango. This should not have surprised them too much, since in English El Lemon means The Lemon. The poverty was not as prevalent and it was decidedly warmer, much hotter than Texas. They had crossed the Tropic of Cancer a few hours before and were now in the tropical area of Mexico. Their excitement was at a fever pitch when they got into the center of the small town. They knew in their spirits that they had found the correct place. Haphazardly parking their El Camino pickup on the side of the street and quickly getting out, James and Phyllis grabbed a handful of tracts and some New Testaments. They were ready to do the work of the Lord. Both of them were so thrilled. As they stood on the dirt sidewalk, their spirits were high and they knew they were where they were supposed to be, but something definitely felt wrong. They had found the town and they were ready to minister, but something just wasn't right. It did not feel right, it did not look right, so they stopped whatever it was they were trying to do. They retreated to the El Camino pickup and again prayed for guidance.

The Word of the Lord came to them, speaking, "Seek the praying man, he will guide you. He will not want to, but insist and he will."

The enemy, Satan, was trying to put doubt in their minds as they asked everyone on the street the location of the "praying man," and all they got was the typical shoulder shrug. Eventually a street vendor said he knew of a praying man and he would tell them if they would purchase some of his goods. He was selling a candy made from squash. Over the years it became one of the family's favorite treats.

Following the confusing directions given by the candy vendor, they finally pulled up to an old, run-down house on the backside of town. There were no vehicles, names, or numbers, just a couple of mongrel dogs laying in the dirt yard. As they were about to enter the yard an older man, obviously an American, came out the front door and cautiously approached them. They visited for a while and the man told his story. He had come down here as a Missionary many years before and had never gone back. His age and health would not let him travel anymore, but he prayed for many of the people in town. He supported himself with a retirement Social Security check from the States and was content never to leave Mexico. He was slightly condescending in his attitude towards the couple, telling them that he had seen many people like them in the past. They had been the wide-eyed visionaries on a mission to save the world, but where were they now? After two weeks, four weeks, or whenever their guilt and conscience had been placated, they were gone. Where were they now? The man seemed cynical and James decided he probably had one oar out of the water. James ignored his attitude and inquired about Laguna. The man laughed and replied that we were the third or fourth wide-eyed visionaries over the years to ask him about Laguna. He said he did not know, but after being pressured, the old man said that he would tell the couple what he had heard.

He sat on a handmade chair and rubbed his chin, saying, "Just as I told the others and then never heard from them again. The roads are bad, and it is too dangerous in those mountains for the likes of you two."

He related the story that had came down out of the mountains by word of mouth, "There was supposedly a small village where some of the inhabitants had been converted to Christianity.

"They are waiting on a Pastor," he said, "and it will be a long wait since nobody knows where this place is or even if it is place. The scuttlebutt is that it is in the top of the mountain range to the west of El Lemon. There are some roads up there, if you can call them that, but mostly just trails. There are plenty of bandits, drug runners, outlaws, and other vermin up there, there's just not much in the way of roads, signs, and the like."

They walked outside and the old man looked at the nearly new El Camino pickup.

"Son," he said, "you won't even get through town in that fancy excuse of truck. Why don't you just go back home now? Don't do anything, just go back and say you did."

James held his tongue as they left the old man to his cynical attitude and drove back across town. He considered his transportation, deciding the old man had been correct. This vehicle was very low to the ground, had chrome exhaust pipes along the outside, a fancy paint job, and chrome trim everywhere. It was a fine, fancy South Texas pickup truck, but not much good for travel on the rough mountain roads of Mexico. They went to a supply store on the highway that serviced the large trucks hauling fruits and vegetables grown in the area. James purchased tools and materials, four containers for gasoline, extra motor oil, etc. Loading the El Camino with all the supplies made it even lower to the ground.

They prayed and drove out of town. About two miles south they came to a fairly well-traveled gravel road that crossed the main highway. It was an area where donkeys pulled carts full of sugar cane to be loaded onto large trucks to travel the highway. Asking if the road going west went to the distant mountains, the answer was, "well, yes and no."

Someone explained that it could go to the mountains as well as other places, but nobody drove there. The laborers said the road stopped in the edge of the low mountains. Riding a donkey or walking was the only way to get to the higher mountains. Then the people laughed and commented that James "sure was riding a fine looking donkey," referring to the fancy El Camino. When asked how to get to Laguna, the people responded with a shrug and a finger pointing toward the blue haze of the distant mountains.

Dark found the couple in the foothills of the mountains. They stopped where a small stream crossed the road, literally crossing over the road. There was a nearly level small spot by the stream and they set up camp. It was a great camp with a pup tent for shelter, an open fire to cook on, and a wonderful star-filled sky for a ceiling. The night was short and certainly not sleep filled. Coyotes howled all night and with the chorus of owls, crickets and other varmints, it was definitely exciting, though not very restful. They had not seen a soul for two hours before stopping and heard no one during the night. They talked long into the night, discussing the changing direction of their lives, and then they finally prayed themselves to sleep.

The next morning they cooked on the open fire and started up the mountains on the unimproved road. Calling this thing a road was really stretching the use of the word road. Trail or path would have been more accurate. After a short time on the road, any evidence that there had ever been another vehicle there at all had vanished. They again prayed and, feeling that they were on the right track, they continued on. The narrow trail was just wide enough for the El Camino, sort of. At times, to negotiate a curve around the steep mountain, it was necessary to put the inside wheels up on the edge of the inside cliff to keep the outside wheels from hanging off the outside cliff. It would have been a good time to turn around and retreat, except there was no room for turning around. After surveying the situation, James realized it would have been impossible to back down the trail. So they continued their slow, steep ascent into the mountains.

About four hours after dark they reached a wide place on the trail that seemed to be fairly level. They could not see where they were or what was in front or behind them. There were no light of any sort visible from their impromptu camping place. They hastily set the tent in the light of the headlights of the truck and slept all night, coyotes or no coyotes. Before dawn the next morning, James was making coffee on the Coleman stove and watching the pitch black night turn into the early morning. He had decided to let Phyllis sleep as late as she could as the previous day had been especially difficult for her. But as daylight came and he surveyed the mountains, he had to wake her up. They stood awestruck at the sight that unfolded before them in the ever-increasing light of dawn.

They were nearly on top of a mountain and had a full one hundred and eighty degree view of the valleys and other smaller mountains below. There was a cliff at the edge of the clearing that must have been thousands of feet straight down. They looked down and saw eagles soaring below them. The area where they had spent the night was solid grass. It looked like a mowed, maintained, and manicured lawn. The grass ran back for a hundred yards or so and continued under a canopy of very large trees. The trees resembled Oaks but James did not think that they were. Growing in the trees were thousands of wild orchids. The colors were purple, yellow, blue, green and every combination of bright colors that could be imagined. Phyllis, after taking a walk in the edge of the forest, commented that she knew they had driven really high yesterday but did not know they had made it to Heaven. They spent a wonderful day at the location and another night in the small tent. James spent part of the day catching up on his journal. The next morning, James did something that was very unusual for him. He felt in his heart that they should continue, but continue where? He stared at the forest and felt they had come to the end of that trail. There was not even a sign of a trail or path, much less a road, which continued past the clearing and into the orchid filled forest. Even though he felt in his heart that he should somehow continue, he chose to listen to his mind, not his heart, and to backtrack. He felt that the most appropriate thing to do was to approach the area from another direction. They would return to El Lemon, and then find a way to circle the mountains and approach from another direction.

Chapter 13

Five days later, after well over a thousand miles of circling the mountains, they had come to a large town by the name of Tula. It was a dark, foreboding and demonic felling place. As they stopped in town to ask directions, the few people that were outside went scurrying back into their nondescript shelters. This was very strange since everywhere else on the trip where they had traveled, all of the people were of the friendliest sort. The streets were nearly deserted and only at the lone, two-pump service station on the highway did anyone even talk with them. They asked the same question they had been asking for nearly a week. Do you know the way to Laguna? The attendant shrugged and pointed towards the distant mountains. The mountains were to the east of Tula. For days they had circled the large mountain range and asked the same question, always receiving the same answer: a shrug of the shoulders and a finger pointed towards the mountains. James drove around the town and found one small gravel road leading across the desert towards the mountains. Two days later on the side of a very rough, single-lane rock road in the middle of nowhere they had a flat tire. It was probably the thirtieth flat since leaving that beautiful spot on top of the mountains where they had camped for two nights..

James had used and ruined his spare and three used tires he had bought on the main highway. He was down to his last package of plugs to fix the flats. Two bars of soap had been used to plug the holes in the gasoline tank of the El Camino that had been caused by the sharp rocks. One of the chrome side pipes had been knocked off and most of the fancy chrome trim had been jarred off. His twelve-volt air compressor used to assist in the flat repair had been rewired many times and by then was on its last leg. It was time to quit and go home, if they could find their way out of this place. Phyllis got out of the truck and joined her husband in prayer. They knelt on the sharp rocks of the so-called road and told God that they had gone as far as they could go. Phyllis did something she had never done before; she pleaded with God to show them a sign if they were to go on.

They continued in prayer for a time and then Phyllis started screaming, "Look, look, oh! Look!"

James opened his eyes and got up off the ground. On the horizon, off to the east, on top of a large hill that would be described better as a small mountain, was an absolutely beautiful, bright, and fully colored rainbow. It was a perfectly clear day, even though it had not rained nor would it rain here for months there was a rainbow. In the very center of the rainbow was a small trail or road going over the mountain.

The Spirit of God spoke to Phyllis and said, "This is my bow, set as a covenant with you."

James repacked his tools yet again and they drove until they found the road they had seen under the rainbow. The rainbow was still there, miles from the first place it had been seen. As they turned onto the non-descript road that went through the center of the rainbow, the rainbow disappeared. Slowly driving up the trail of a road towards the top of the small mountain, they finally reached the top. As they crossed over the top, down below on the other side was a village with a relative large body of water beside it. Large for this area anyway, for this was the desert and there was not supposed to be any lakes or ponds; but there one was.

James stopped the vehicle and started to weep, then explained to his wife, "Honey, do you know what 'Laguna' means, it means 'the lagoon' or lake. We have found the place God sent us to find. This has to be Laguna."

They eased the vehicle down the steep trail to the small village below. There were no signs, no service stations, and only one place that looked as thought it might be selling something. They found out later that it was a 'Conosupo', a very small grocery store of sorts. They turned off to the left on what could best be called an unimproved dirt street. James stated that he felt in his spirit that this was the way they were expected to go. The street ended in about one hundred yards, and cacti, a few loose goats, and more cacti were the only things in front of them. After driving a zigzag course around the cacti for about one quarter of a mile, they came to a stick fence. There was a small mud-brick building on the other side of the fence. James stopped the badly damaged El Camino pickup and announced to his wife that they had made it to their destination. Phyllis was having some concern about the pronouncement, and probably more concern about the mental state of her husband, but she got out of the vehicle and walked with him to the fence. As they approached the fence, from the opposite side, a small group of people came out of a small mud-brick structure. They were mostly older, with one exception, a young woman, probably in her late twenties. The group came to a gate in the fence, opened it, and invited the visitors inside.

When they were all inside gate, the young woman with the group asked the visitors "Are you the pastor? We have been waiting for so long for the Pastor, are you the one?"

James responded that he was a minister but did not think he was going to be their Pastor. The visitors were welcomed into the mud-brick building and the history of those gathered there was recounted by a young woman. The young woman, whose name was Juanita, introduced herself and the others, and then told the history of the building and the reason the folks gathered there.

About seven years before, some of the villagers went to the city of Victoria, a relatively large and modern city two hundred miles to the north. They had gone to visit some relatives and to celebrate Holy Week (Easter week, which is a national holiday in Mexico). While in the city, some of them attended an evangelical tent meeting. They were led to the Lord and told by the leader of the group holding the meeting to go back to the mountains, build a Church, and a Pastor would come. They did as instructed and had been waiting for nearly seven years for the promised man of God to come and teach them. They had brought back one Bible from the city and it lay on top of a small table that was covered with a beautiful white hand-crocheted cover. They gathered daily after their work had been done, and whenever possible, to listen as the young woman, Juanita, read from the Bible. She was the only one of the group who could read and she used this talent to help the others hear the Word of God.

During the ensuing hours of conversation the subject of prayer came up. They told Jim that mostly they just read and listened to the reading of the Bible. They also stated that they did not pray much here, only at home. When inquired as to why they did not pray much here in the building they had dedicated as a

Church, Juanita responded by asking if their guest would like to lead them in prayer. James asked if he should pray in Spanish or English.

One of the elderly men replied, "It doesn't matter to God does it? He speaks both languages, right."

James thought he had came here to Mexico to teach, but realized he really came to learn from the wisdom and dry humor of these wonderful people.

They all gathered around the table with the Bible on it and James began to pray. As he started, he noticed that all the people were looking at each other with fleeting and cautious glances; undeterred by this he continued. A roaring noise distracted James. Then the noise became very loud and a fierce wind began to blow, or so it seemed. The noise was there, but there was no wind. He was forced to raise his voice to a very loud volume to speak above the sound of the wind. At the same time the animals first became restless and then began fighting each other: dogs, chickens, pigs, donkeys and others. What had been a calm late afternoon turned into utter chaos. It did not take a lot of snap for anyone to recognize this as a demonic attack, so stepping out of the Church James took authority over the situation.

Recalling from the fourth chapter of Mark in the New Testament, where Jesus took authority over the wind and the waves, James commanded, in the Name of Jesus Christ, for peace to return. After the third time he spoke to the turmoil, peace returned. James returned inside to the see the astonished faces of the local Believers. After he finished his prayer, they all began to smile and shake his hand and pat him on the shoulder. They asked over and over if he was sure that he was not the Pastor. Then they related that every time they tried to join together in prayer, the same thing happened, but, Glory to God, today they were all going to pray together. The entire group stayed for services that night, followed by a wonderful meal of black beans and corn tortillas. They all visited late into the night. The main topic was that of the Believers needing a spiritual leader. James was positive that it was not him, for he knew he was to go to a place called San Mateo. He did, however, feel a great responsibility to help in any way that he could. He promised the Believers that he would find a Pastor and send him to them. They all rejoiced in the Lord and prayed until very late that night. The sounds of the non-existent winds did not interfere.

The next day, while exploring the village, Phyllis and James found a really nice looking two-lane improved rock road leading out of town. It started out the back side of town and the road could not be seen until you walked right up to it. He inquired at the Church a little later as to where the road went and was told it went nowhere, only to the top of the mountains and then it stopped. The villagers then inquired as to whether the visitors would like to go there, excitedly tell the American couple that it was a most beautiful spot. The plans were made and after breakfast the next morning, the El Camino was loaded with people and they started up the road. The eldest man, Lionel, rode in the front with James while Phyllis, and five other ladies rode in the back. This was one custom that Phyllis was not too happy about, but she smiled and climbed into the back of the pickup. The road was surprisingly level and wide, it rose higher and higher up into the mountains. The landscape there was barren, and even barren does not truly describe it. High mountain desert with no trees or grass and only cacti greeted them as they drove. The elderly man, Lionel, told James that the government was building this road and it was supposed to go from Tula, where Jim had last filled the pickup and the spare cans with gas, to the other side of the mountains. This short section, here in the middle of nowhere, was all that had been completed. As they reached the end of the road, a very abrupt end, the view was great.

They walked over the ridge of the mountain crest and on the other side it was green, not just some green, but all green. Looking to the west it was brown and sand colored, but turning around and looking to the east, it was as green as a jungle. They were on the continental divide and to the east was the Gulf of Mexico, with rain, moisture, and green. To the west was dry and desert. As the wet winds and clouds came in off the gulf, they would get to the top of these mountains. There, the dry winds from the desert would blow back towards the gulf. This had the effect of making one side of the mountains a rain forest and the other side a barren desert. Lionel and his daughter walked with the visitors toward some really large trees at the edge of the green side of the mountain.

As they approached the trees Jim suddenly realized where they were. He ran through the orchid filled trees for about two hundred yards to the other side of the small forest and there was the grassy flat where, over a week before, Phyllis and he had spent two wonderful nights at their makeshift camp. This was the place they had stopped before going back down the mountain to El Lemon. He was shocked. Phyllis was shocked. They had their picnic that day at the same place they had previously camped and headed back down the mountain. According to the odometer and his watch, James decided it was seven miles and twenty minutes back to the church in Laguna. A week before, they had been seven miles and twenty minutes from their destination, when Jim had decided to retreat and not to go on. He had felt in his spirit that he should continue but could see nothing to continue on. He realized that he did not see a way to continue because he was not looking for one. He had been caught in the trap of looking at the circumstances and not at the goal. All he could see were the trees. Had he just went and looked; he would have found the way God had sent him. James promised himself and God that he would never go by sight again, but only by faith as he was led by the Spirit of God.

After holding services for a third night, plans were made to return in thirty days and to hold a baptismal service for the church as none of the Believers had yet been baptized. Before they left, they prayed, without the howling wind, wept, and professed their love for the newly found Brethren. James restated his promise concerning finding a Pastor and then he and Phyllis started back to Texas. Once they reached Tula, refueled, and got on the main highway, the travel became much easier. The highway circled the mountains and after one hundred and fifty miles it connected to another main highway that eventually connected to the one they had started on well over a week before. They were exhausted but joyful. The trip was deemed a near success. The only thing was they still did not know where San Mateo was located. When he was leaving Laguna, James had asked where San Mateo was and received the typical negative shoulder shrug.

Chapter 14

The month spent waiting for the next trip to Mexico was a joyful experience of sharing the events that had happened on the first trip, and looking forward to and preparing for the next trip. Though he knew he had been thoroughly blessed by all that took place, James only came to the knowledge of how much of a blessing it was when he shared the experience with others. It was during those times that he would break down and cry in the middle of relating one incident or another. It was a nearly impossible to make it through relating his experiences without his voice starting to crack and tears welling up in his eyes. His and his wife's lives had forever been changed by the experience, and that change was definitely for the better.

Of all the things that happened during that month of waiting, one event stands out above all the rest. James was going to the mall to meet a Pastor friend for lunch. After parking, he was walking to the main entrance, enjoying an impromptu conversation with some "Winter Texans," retirees from the northern part of the United States that spend the colder winter months in South Texas because of the warm climate. They were asking many questions about the area and possible activities in which they might participate. As the group neared the main entrance to the mall, a small, very elderly woman came bursting out of the doors; her hair was disheveled, she was walking strangely, and she started to scream at James.

"Who do you think you are? Who do you think you are? You stupid human, coming here to the mountains with your so called spirituality, who do you think you are?" She turned her head at an almost impossible angle and continued, "We have had these mountains for thousands of years and you come strolling down here like you're somebody!" She began shaking and screamed even louder, "If you come back you will be killed, you and your family will die a slow horrid death. Do you hear me? Do you?"

James was reminded of the events in the sixteenth chapter of the Book of Acts, when the possessed slave girl was harassing Paul. In that account, Paul takes authority over the demon and brings calm to the situation. James felt that if it corrected the situation then, it would correct the situation now.

James raised his hand towards the distraught woman and commanded, "You foul evil spirit, cease and desist. I am a servant of the Lord Jesus Christ and I command you by the blood of that self same Jesus!"

The woman screamed even louder, "Damn you, damn you, damn you!"

She then hiked up her skirt and ran out through the parking lot at a surprisingly fast pace, way too fast for an old woman. She came to the guardrail on the expressway, jumped over it, and disappeared in the distance.

James turned to the "Winter Texans" and asked, "Have you nice folks found a church to attend while you are visiting here?"

The Winter Texans were wide-eyed as James held the door open for them. They were also very quiet as they scurried through the door.

Jim thought, "I don't think it would do any good to invite them to our church."

At lunch as he and his Pastor friend discussed the incident, they were both amazed that a local evil spirit had communicated with someone from the mountains of Mexico. They also discussed the possibility that the demon had come from the mountains in Mexico, possible with Phyllis and James when they returned. Now that was a scary thought. Before leaving each other's company that day, they had a long sincere prayer for the elderly lady that had been used by the demon, and for the "Winter Texans" to get through their experience of earlier that day.

As the time for the next trip south approached, James did not have much of a clue about how to go about the trip. All he knew was that he had promised to return to Laguna for a baptism service on a particular day. He supposed he would spend the rest of the trip searching for the seemingly non-existent village of San Mateo. The night before leaving for Mexico, the vehicle was packed, the paperwork readied, and the couple was very excited. They had borrowed a van, one that a friend had fixed up for hunting with extra gas tanks and considerable ground clearance, and they had much more confidence in that vehicle than in the El Camino. As Jim looked at the maps to try to find a closer route to Laguna, he took a Marks-a-Lot and drew the last trip on the map. He had a map of the northern half of Mexico with a large, nearly perfect, circle drawn on it. He commented that they had drove in a giant circle all over northern Mexico during the last trip to find the small village of Laguna, with its mud-brick church and handful of very dedicated Believers. Neither Laguna, nor the roads going to it, were on the map, but he did remember in what general area of the mountain range it was located and he plotted it on the map.

As he searched the map, James began to pray and ask for guidance for their new adventure.

It was as though the Spirit of the Lord was saying, "I have already instructed you."

As his diary was packed in the car, he asked Phyllis if she could find his journal with the notes they had made the night of the prayer meetings two years before. She could, as she was the organized one of the pair; they were in her Bible. Phyllis's Bible and the container she carried it in contained not only the Word of God, but also notes, paper, pictures, birth certificates, James' journal, and anything else they might ever need for any situation. As he read the notes, the last sentence on the paper he had filled out and the next to the last sentence on the paper Phyllis filled out leaped off the page at him. 'The place is in the middle of the circle'.

Dear God, James thought, thank you, thank you, and thank you. He put the map on the coffee table and found a drawing compass from his desk. He found the exact center of the circle they had drove on the previous trip and announced to Phyllis that he knew where San Mateo was located. This is where we are going to live. This is where we are to minister. His wife looked at the large blank spot on the map with the little x drawn on it. No roads, no rivers, no towns, no names, just a large blank space with an x.

She looked at him with that knowing smile that wives develop, and said, "Maybe, maybe not, but I did say I would follow you wherever."

By sunrise the next morning, they were well on the way into Mexico. Jim had brought the map with the blank spot and the x, a directional sight compass, dividers, and other navigational aids. They had three and a half days before they were to be at Laguna for the baptism service and he was bound and determined to find San Mateo. It was well after dark when they were as close, at least as close as James could determine, to the x as the main road came. They turned off the main road onto a small, extremely narrow, one-lane path of a roadway, without signs. As they drove deeper into an unknown area in the dark of the night, his excitement grew. When they would come to a split in the road, he would choose the direction indicated by the hand-held compass that was toward the center of the circle on the map. It was after midnight when they pulled off to the side of the road and used the back of the van for a bed.

As the sun rose the next morning, James prepared coffee and breakfast on the Coleman stove and surveyed the area. He didn't have a clue where he was. The night before, they had spent several hours in the dark on crooked mountain roads while making at least ten turns off the previous road they were traveling on. He tried to estimate the distance between the turns, and the directions of those turns, and to determine his present location. He only knew that he was inside of the circle on the map, and he felt that they were on the path they should be on. As they were finishing breakfast and preparing to continue, a man rode by on a donkey. James offered coffee and breakfast, which the man readily accepted.

When asked if he knew where San Mateo was, the man's answer was, "no," with the customary shoulder shrug.

He did tell the couple that they were crazy for being out in this part of the country, especially at night. "Banditos y Drugistas," he proclaimed (bandits and drug runners). "They would love to have your vehicle," he professed with many hand gestures.

Ignoring this negativity, James made the man another cup of coffee and shared the gospel of Christ with him. The man got on his knees and gloriously accepted Jesus Christ as his Savior.. James gave the man a Spanish New Testament and felt that the trip had already been a success. They kept on their jagged path across the high desert and into the mountains. Phyllis shared with James that the night before, God had given her a dream about a really small church and seven Christians waiting for them. They prayed, rejoiced, and drove on and on.

They came upon a small town of about two hundred dwellings. No signs, no names, just a town. Stopping and asking for directions to San Mateo, all they got were blank stares and shrugged shoulders. They did find a man who had some barrels of gasoline in his back yard. The fuel was for sale and, this being the only resemblance of a gas station, they filled both their vehicle's fuel tanks. While paying the man for the fuel, James again inquired about San Mateo. The man replied that he had been here for his whole life and that there was no town, village, or even a ranch named San Mateo. They got no directions to San Mateo, but the travelers did buy some tacos to eat later on that day. James was not deterred and with full fuel tanks he steadfastly continued to where he thought the x would be found. They did find out that the town, where they stopped and had gotten the gas and tacos, was named Lleno.

In the mid-afternoon and only about ten miles and two hours from where they had gotten gas, a small dirt and rock road led up to the left. The road or path looked un-traveled and nearly abandoned. A barbed wire gate blocked the road and there were no indications where it might lead. They stopped and ate the tacos, and James studied the map and prayed. Declaring that this was the road, he opened the barbed wire gate, passed through, and closed it behind them. Passing through a closed gate was not a wise thing to do, neither in Texas nor in Mexico, but James just knew that this was the way. The road, and calling this thing a road was really being kind, started climbing up the side of the largest mountain that could be seen in the entire mountain range. In many places, the trail was not wide enough for the vehicle and the inside wheels were placed up on the inside cliffs as had to be done on the first trip. The drop-offs, just inches from the outside wheels, seemed to go straight down forever. Again it was impossible to turn around, so they drove on and up. The steepness of the climb was causing the transmission and engine to overheat, but there was really no other choice except to wait for it to cool, then to continue. The higher clearance of the van and the extra gas tanks were an advantage, but he would have to do better in the future. Without any prior indication, the road made a sharp right turn around an outcropping, then flattened and came to an end.

In front of them was a small village. It could not be seen from anywhere on the road up, but there it was. A number of small huts were located around an empty area, with more huts scattered up the side of the mountain. The empty area was about the size of a football field and they later found out it was used for soccer and/or impromptu rodeos. After the terrifying climb up the mountain, the beauty, peace, and serenity of this place felt absolutely amazing. The towering mountain that continuined up behind the village, the vast valleys below, the eagles circling in the air, and the mist rising from the lower valleys were all beautiful beyond description. James believed they had found their destination and he stopped the tired van in the center of the field. They sat there for a few moments and surveyed this paradise. Phyllis let out a yell and started talking so fast that she could hardly be understood.

"Look, look, there it is, there it is," she proclaimed.

At the upper end of the empty field, about fifty yards away, was a really small building with a group of people standing outside.

"Honey, that's the church I saw in my dream last night," she said, with such excitement she could hardly be understood.

They prayed and thanked God for the safe journey, exited the vehicle, and started up and across the field toward the small building. Right away, they realized the the air was thin as they walked the inclined field. They would later learn that they were at eight thousand feet above sea level. Huffing and puffing, they made their way to the small building. It was strange that there were no other people to be seen. At the building, they stopped in front of the group that was standing there.

Phyllis was looking at the ground, not the people, and asking, "How many are there, how many are there?"

Her husband looked and replied, "How many did you expect?"

She looked at James with a look that said: "Did you come to town on a potato wagon?"

She then reminded her husband about the dream of the small church and the seven people. There were only six people standing by the low opening of the small building. Phyllis was disappointed, but was also so excited that no one could tell.
The six people cautiously examined the Americans and asked, "Are you the Pastor?"

James and Phyllis were awestruck.

They were even more amazed when another young man came walking up through the back side of the village and said, "God spoke to me at my village last night and said there would be a Pastor here today, are you the one?"

The man had walked for eight hours to get there. He was part of the family that formed this group of Believers but he lived on a ranch in the mountains. That made seven people waiting for them at the church. Phyllis was ecstatic and everybody began talking at once. After some time, James ascertained what had taken place in this remote mountain village. The local Christians had been banned from publicly displaying their faith. They had been praying privately for someone to come that could change that situation. God had spoken to them saying that today was the day, and they had gathered to wait. They went inside the small building and James began to weep and to praise God for His unlimited mercy and faithfulness. The locals joined in and there was an enthusiastic prayer meeting.

Later James was accompanied by one of the men to visit the Mayor of the village. When asked for permission to hold a church service, the man was reluctant, but he agreed with the stipulation that they could not invite anyone. If someone wanted to attend, he would not stop them, but the Christians had to remain in their building, without visiting any homes except their own. James was grateful and would take what he could get. The afternoon blended into the evening and it was all like a dream to James and his wife. The service was fantastic, the building filled with many being saved and many more asking for prayer for healing. The prevailing health problem was a skin infection on the children, a really terrible looking malady. The prayer for healing was offered for the dozens afflicted, and hands were laid on each one as they were anointed with oil. The little building was literally overflowing with the curious. The outside was crowded with villagers trying to get a peek in the one door or through one of the small open windows. Late into the night after the service had run its course, some of the attendees brought food for the visitors to eat. Afterwards they made pallets on the dirt floor of the church for beds, they were very exhausted and laid down shortly..

After the village had quieted and the animal noise was down to a low roar, James reached over and took his wife's hand and thanked her for standing by him on this venture. They prayed thankfully for the trip, the service, their safety, and for this place. When inquiring if this was really San Mateo earlier in the evening, he had been told that this was in fact San Mateo.

"But nobody has ever heard of it," James responded.

The locals laughed and explained the old name of the village was Santa Lucia, but a few years ago the government, for whatever reason, had changed it to San Mateo. Every one still refers to the place as Santa Lucia. They told the American he was correct that no one knew where San Mateo was, but it was right here. As they drifted off to sleep to the serenade of donkeys braying and pigs grunting, the uniqueness of the events in their lives became so very real, so very overwhelming, and they were so grateful.

The next morning they obtained directions to Laguna from where they were. It was only about twenty-five miles but it would take more than six hours to negotiate the camelback turns and steep grades. Before leaving San Mateo, they made arrangements to return the next day for another visit. Driving carefully down the steep grade to the dirt road in the valley, they were stopped by the Mayor, who was waiting for them on the steep grade. He did not want anyone to see him conversing with the Americans, so he had walked part of the way down the mountain to an area that could not be seen from the village. He had heard of the healings the night before and brought his son with him. The boy was about seven-years-old and nearly covered with a rash that had many areas of sores and scabs. The Mayor ordered them to fix the boy, and not to tell anyone. Totally ignoring the man's attitude and situation, James laid hands on the boy and prayed for him to be healed and for the healing to bring glory to God and faith to the people. As they continued down the steep grade on the way to Laguna, the 'Mayor' took a back way to the village to keep his visit a secret.

Thirty hours later they were going back up the steep grade to San Mateo. The services in Laguna had been fantastic, with many saved and many baptized. They had left before sun-up and were now near the end of another arduous six-hour drive. As they pulled into the field in the center of the village there were probably two hundred people gathered there. Standing in front of them was the Mayor. He was standing with his hand on his son's shoulder. The boy, who one day earlier had scabs and open sores all over his body, was totally healed. No sign of the rash was to be seen on any of his exposed body, not even one sore or scar. All the other children were the same. This boy and all of the other children that had been prayed for were totally set free from the skin infections and sores.

"Praise God! Praise God! Praise God!" shouted James and Phyllis.

Getting on his knees, James gathered the children around him and rejoiced in the Spirit. The Mayor stood there as proud as could be, no longer ashamed to associate with these strangers. The story of 'the healing of the children' spread quickly and widely throughout the mountains. James was sure that the events had happened in that fashion to establish him and Phyllis as true representatives of God.

In the spiritual realm the events that had been and were happening on the mountain were dutifully relayed to Somne Octe by some of the underlings that were on assignment in the area around San Mateo.

"Not to be concerned," Somne Octe replied, "These stupid humans as with all who have tried before to invade my territory, will be dealt with and will be of no consequence, and they will not return." Somne Octe spoke with authority and confidence, fully aware of his power and position in this area of the world.

A late afternoon service was held. It was a time of rejoicing, singing, praying, preaching, and fellowship between the residents of this far away place and the visitors God had sent them. James was on a spiritual high like he had never experienced. Everything was working just as it was supposed to work. The Word of God was being preached and people were being saved, with hands lain on the sick and prayers offered, and there were many healings. James had retrieved his guitar from the vehicle and was joined by a half dozen other instrument-playing villagers. It was the apex of James' spiritual experience and he and his wife were absolutely ecstatic. The time came for them to depart and start the overnight drive back to the states. As they were saying their goodbyes, an older woman asked if they could pray for her niece. James consulted with Phyllis and decided to honor the request, even though the time was short. He then asked the Mayor for permission and it was readily given. They were informed that they would have to walk to the highest compound in the village. The house was at the top of the village on the side of the mountain. It was a steep and difficult climb for them, as they were not yet acclimated to the atmosphere of the high altitude. James noticed that none of the other villagers came with them.

"Strange," he thought, "I wonder why?"

Chapter 15

As they neared the huts at the end of the steep trail, two really large, extremely violent and angry dogs came running at them. The old woman, who was leading them, took her walking stick and readied herself to fight off the animals.

James stepped forward, stretched out his clinched fist and commanded, "In the name of Jesus Christ, I order you to cease, be calm, and leave. You will bring us no harm as we are servants of the Most High God."

The dogs stopped in their tracks, started to whimper, and ran in the opposite direction.

James looked at his wife, smiled and said, "At the name of Christ, every knee shall bow."

The older woman looked at them and said, "Huh!" with a lot of disdain.

She did not seem to be overly impressed. James had never been arrogant about his faith or his God given gifts, but he was feeling really good right about then.

As they entered the compound, the woman was asked where the niece was and what was wrong with her. The woman pointed with her walking cane at a low-lying mud hut with a thatch roof, set at the rear of the collection of huts. She stated that the girl suffered from "malevida". Phyllis inquired of her husband what specifically that was and he said he did not have a clue, but would guess it means something about a bad life or something close to that. He was wishing his Spanish were better and that he understood the local slang words. As they approached the hut, the door astonished him. It was a large, heavy, wooden door, not like the flimsy stick ones he had noticed on the other buildings. Against it, a pile of large rocks held it in place. Tying the door closed was the largest rope he had ever seen, other than on a shrimp boat. The woman busied herself untying the rope and moving the rocks, and James and Phyllis wondered what they had gotten themselves into.

When the door was pulled back, James realized that there were no windows and the place was as dark as a cave. He started in but was overcome by the stench of the place that wafted out of the doorway. After a few moments he entered and his wife followed. As his eyes grew accustomed to the dark interior, he saw a cot against one of the walls. With the small amount of light that came in through the doorway, and his eyes adjusting to the darkness, he was able to make out the form of someone lying on the cot. He cautiously stepped over to the cot. His head was bumping the thatch roof and he had to bend over as he stood and stared down at the figure on the cot.

James was totally surprised and shocked by what he saw. There was a young girl lying on the cot. Her eyes were wide open, her hair was matted, her face swollen, and a loosely woven horsehair blanket covered her. She was obviously naked beneath the blanket and her hands were clasped around her own throat. The fingernails on her filthy hands were a full three inches long and, as he would later learn, had been growing since she was locked in the building years earlier. Her legs extended from under the blanket above the ankles, down to her feet. That part of her anatomy was especially clean compared to the rest of her body. She appeared not to be breathing, but upon close examination she was taking very shallow breaths. James' mind raced, searching for a feasible explanation for this situation; he did not have much success. As he stared at he girl, a flicker of recognition rose in his mind. He nearly dropped his Bible to the filthy floor as he realized who this girl was; without a doubt this was the girl from the dream two years before, the same one from the vision a year past. Her hair was a total mess and her face was oddly swollen but this was the same person. The girl from the visions who had reached out to James twice and asked for his help!

He spoke out, "My God, my God, my God, please help me. Please show me what this means. Please show me what I am supposed to do."

James looked at his wife and told her what he had realized. This was the girl of whom he had spoken. He instructed his wife to tell him when two hours were up, since they had to start back to Texas.

He then stated, though not from his thought patterns, but from the Spirit of God, "She is possessed and we are here to free her. This is what the Angel was talking about when he visited me on the oil lease. She is the one in the dream; she is the one in the vision. Phyllis, this is what the prophetic words over the last four years have been about!"

An excitement rose up inside of him as he surveyed his surroundings, trying to decide what to do. He knew through the Name of Jesus, and through James' belief in Christ as the Son of God, that he had the authority over demons. James remembered the old woman at the mall and the dogs just a few moments ago; yes, he had the authority. He had prayed for people to be delivered from this or that, commanding the offending spirit to leave, but this was a decidedly different situation.

After composing himself, James recalled the scriptures that had to do with Christ freeing those being held captive by demons. Jesus commanded the demons to come out and release the person and the demons obeyed. He also recalled the passage in the fourteenth chapter of John, where Jesus said that Believers could do all the things that Jesus had done. There was plenty of scripture that covered the authority of the Believer to use the name of Jesus in circumstances such as these. James could not stand up straight as the roof was too low and there was no chair or bench to sit on. His one choice was to kneel beside the cot on the filthy floor. James kept thinking that he would get used to the stench, but that was not to be the case. The roughly made cot, just a frame really, had a mattress of sorts made from a woven rope material. It was absolutely soaked with stale urine and the heat and the high humidity only intensified the odor.

Trying his best to ignore the smell, he requested that his wife pray and be supportive in what was going to take place. He again prayed for guidance, and with full confidence he approached the task that was set before him, to set the captive free. He started to pray and to command the evil spirits to flee. Over and over he did this in every way he had read or heard about regarding situations such as this. Nothing happened, absolutely nothing.

James continued, again and again attempting to take authority without results. After an hour his legs and back had begun to cramp and he stood up the best that he could. He then leaned over the cot and placed one hand against the mud wall across the cot from him for support. As he did this, the Bible he was holding in the other hand came very close to the girl's open eyes. The girl screamed, though scream doesn't describe the sound that came out of her. It was more like the roar of a mountain lion or a panther. To say it startled James and his wife would be a gross understatement. But outside the hut, the aunt was dancing around for joy, as it was the first time Sara had moved or spoken in over a year. Sara closed her hands tighter around her throat and tried to choke herself. James, while continuing to pray, grabbed her wrist and tried desperately to pull her hands away from her throat. It seemed he was not going to be able to stop the choking but finally he broke the death grip and her hands relaxed. He quit praying for her to stop choking and returned to a prayer of petition to know what to do.

James moved back a step and waited until his ears stopped ringing from the roar. Then he tried to sort out what was happening. It is almost impossible to express the disappointment, concern, and confusion that churned inside of him. He had repeatedly done what he thought the Bible instructed and got nothing but a panther's roar that nearly gave him a stroke. Doggedly, he decided to continue with the only thing he knew to do. He moved around to the head of the cot and commenced to pray again. Sara's eyes rolled back in her head and she arched her neck to better see who was disturbing her. She looked straight into James' eyes.

She screamed, in English, with a definite Cajun accent, "You're killing me you son of a bitch, you're killing me." James wondered where she learned English, but would find out later that she only spoke Spanish.

Then there was silence, without movement, for another thirty minutes. James inquired of his wife what the time was. She responded that it was past time for them to leave for the States. He prayed a few more moments and decided that he had no choice but to leave. Walking down the hill towards their vehicle, the aunt filled them in on the history of the girl, at least what she knew of it. Her name was Sara. Her cheeks were swollen from the forced feeding, and until today she had not moved in well over a year. The old woman, the aunt that had brought them to see Sara, was jubilant over what had taken place, but James was sad and confused, actually felling defeated. He promised the aunt and the people in the village that he would return in a month. The Mayor gave James a hug, slapped him on the back three times, and told him they would be waiting.

James and Phyllis were exhausted as they headed north on the long road to Texas. As the miles and hours rolled by, James was very quiet for most of the journey. They crossed the border into the United States just at sunrise, and then he became very talkative.

"The scriptures say that sometimes these evil spirits only go forth by fasting and prayer," he said with a dry, husky, and tired voice.

He went on to explain that he was going to spend the next month fasting, praying, and reading the Bible, and he wanted Phyllis to run the business for him. She readily agreed.

"There was something drastically wrong with that situation yesterday. It cannot be with God, it cannot be with Jesus Christ, it cannot be with the Holy Spirit, so therefore it has to be with me and my interpretation of the Word of God. I will fast and seek the truth of the Word until we return to Mexico," he declared firmly.

The month passed relatively quickly with Phyllis dividing her time between the service business and the children, and with her husband praying, fasting, and reading the Word. James ate no food and drank only water for the 30 days. It never ceased to amaze him that when he read the Word for the Word's sake, not filtered through the lens of one doctrine or another, how wonderfully clear it was. The Written Word of Almighty God just comes alive when accepted for what it is. He came to realize during the month that, all too often, we come to the Word for what we want it to say, from some pre-conceived idea or position. For thirty days James only wanted the Word to speak to his spirit, and the Word definitely spoke…

He started the month with the scripture from the First Epistle of John, reading the second chapter's twenty-sixth and twenty-seventh verses:

"*These things I have written to you concerning those who try to deceive you. But the anointing which you have received from Him abides in you, and you do not need that anyone teach; but as the same anointing teaches you concerning all things, and is true, and is not a lie, and just as it has taught you, you will abide in Him.*"

It was so simple to read the Word and let the Holy Spirit do the teaching. Throw away all the other books, the second-hand scriptures, and go to the source. The Word would be taught by the Holy Spirit and would be all truth and no lie. Even though he had been a Bible student all his life, even when he was running from his calling, this month would be a fantastic time of learning and renewing.

First, James re-researched the authority given to Believers. In the interest of space I will not go into the whole month's study, but I do want to include the highlights:

James went to the fourteenth chapter of John, verses twelve through fourteen:

"Most sincerely I (Jesus) say unto you, he who believes in me, the things that I do he will be able to do also; and even greater things than these he will be able to do, because I go to My Father. Anything you ask in My Name, I will do it for you, so that My Father in Heaven may be glorified in the Son. What you ask for in My Name (the Name of Jesus); it will be done."

He rejoiced in the Spirit at this revelation of authority for the Believer. He had read it many times but this time it was as though the words were leaping off the page.

He balanced this with John, chapter five, verses fourteen and fifteen:

"This is the faith (confidence) that we (Believers) have in Him (God). Anything that we pray within His will, He will hear the request. We also know that if He hears us, we (Believers) will have what we request."

As the Holy Spirit showed James the flow of the scriptures, it became really simple to understand the revelations. It became clear: be a true Believer, know the will of God, ask within that will, ask in the Name of Jesus, and you will get the request. Could it really be that simple? Yes, it could, and is, and will be.

The situation facing James was of course one of casting out a demon and freeing a prisoner, so he looked into that specific area of the Scripture. In the fourth chapter of Luke, verse eighteen, he read, *"God has sent Me (Jesus) to heal the brokenhearted...to preach deliverance to the captives...to set at liberty those who are oppressed..."*

In the sixteenth chapter of Mark, verses fifteen through eighteen, he read:

"Go to the whole world and preach the Good News to every person. Those that believe and are baptized will be saved. And those who do not believe will not be saved but condemned. These are the signs that well follow the True Believers: In my name they will cast out demons, they will speak with other tongues, they will take up snakes, and if they drink things that are deadly they will not be hurt. The True Believer will lay hands on the sick and they will be healed."

In the tenth chapter of Acts, verse thirty-eight, James read:

"How God anointed Jesus of Nazareth with the power of the Holy Spirit, who (Jesus) went around doing good and healing all who were oppressed by the devil; for God was with Him."

He studied, memorized, and prayed over these and many other passages concerning the freedom from demonic oppression and the authority of the True Believer. He also put into his memory every passage in which Jesus confronted the demons and cast them out. Out of all the studies that James did during the month of fasting was, the study that impressed him most was when Satan himself was confronting and tempting Jesus after the forty day fast. Jesus used only scripture to totally defeat the Satan, not trickery, not fancy language, not gimmicks, just the ever truthful, living, absolute Word of God. This was a lesson to be learned and meditated on for days to fully assimilate the deep hidden truths which was becoming so clear in James' mind.

Towards the end of the month of fasting and study when James took a bread and was reading the story about the Little Engine That Could to his daughters, the Spirit reminded him about determination, faith, and perseverance. It was a cute story for the children, but the full truth of the story would become so very evident in his life over the next few months.

Chapter 16

One month after the first trip to the Village of San Mateo.

James and Phyllis had borrowed a different van for this trip, and it bounced and slid, and moaned and groaned, as it climbed the dirt road up the side of the mountain to San Mateo. Calling this glorified cow trail a road was still really a stretch. The incline in some places was nearly 40 degrees and the width was not made for a full sized vehicle. The particular van had much more cargo space, but it gave up a lot in agility. Parts of the road were so narrow that with the vehicle against cliff on the inside, the tires on the outside were not fully on the road; James had to back up a little and try to change the angle of the approach. He realized that this was not the type of vehicle that he needed for these mountains either. It took much prayer and careful driving on the seven miles of really bad road up Mount Jefe to get to the village. Bouncing to a stop at the base of the village, James could see most of the twenty-four family compounds, and it was as beautiful as remembered. There was the normal amount of activity going on in the place, but there was also strangeness in the air. All the inhabitants knew that the American was coming today to pray for Sara, and they were afraid of what evil the spirits might release on the village.

There had been meetings over the previous month to decide whether to let the Americans come back to the village or not. Those most fearful of the Witches were in favor of banning the "gringos" from returning, but the others had won out. They had won out not by numbers but rather by reasoning. This was real democracy at work. The ones not in favor of a ban had put forth the proposition that James and his wife had brought no harm, and had asked nothing of the villagers. Just the opposite, they had brought clothes and staples and other things as gifts, and had asked for nothing in return. The village children had been cured of the dreaded skin diseases. The position was that you could not condemn someone for something that might take place, only for a wrong that had already taken place. After due consideration, all agreed not to stop the Americans from returning.

James and Phyllis made the obligatory visits with the town leaders and the Christian family that had welcomed them before. After the cursory visits, they started up the mountain with a number of villagers to where Sara was locked in the mud hut. James had forgotten how thin the air was here high on the side of the 13,000 ft. mountain and was wishing he had more help with the supplies he had brought. The backpacks contained a Coleman lantern and fuel, and many dozens of large candles. The ice chest had Mexico Coca-Colas and American protein bars. The ice chest was heavy, seemingly even more so because of the extreme altitude. The steep climb was finally negotiated and they stood at the handmade gate in front of the compound. This time the dogs paid them no attention and the only member of Sara's family that came out to meet them was the aunt.

One could not say they were welcomed in; instead, they were just barely permitted to be there. The attitude of the family was a concern to James and later he would realize why. They were escorted back to the low, windowless mud structure. The door was still blocked by large rocks and tied with that very large rope. The small opening in the four-foot high door was still covered over from the outside. This of course meant that the inside would be in total darkness. It took nearly thirty minutes to move the rocks and free the door. As Jim moved the door so they could enter, the stench that rushed out through the opening was fully as overwhelming as it was on the prior visit. Waiting a few moments before entering, hoping that the smell would become bearable, and the handful of Christians who had followed the American up the mountain gathered around the hut and entered into prayer.

James was thinking that it was kind of a milquetoast type of prayer that probably did not shake the portals of Heaven, but he knew it came out of sincere hearts. He also knew that what he was about to embark on was the pinnacle of four years of preparation. Today was the day that had been prophesied. Today was the reason the Angel had visited him. Today was why he had been brought from a life of sin into a life of serving God. He was apprehensive about his abilities, but his faith in God through Jesus Christ was at an all time high. He had no idea what to expect, he only knew that he was supposed to be there. This was a God-given destiny and whatever happened would be in the hands of that self-same God.

Entering the low mud-brick structure and trying to breathe as shallowly as possible to handle the stench, James let his eyes grow accustomed to the darkness. He did not even glance towards the handmade cot. He and the others placed candles around the room and lit them to bring at least a small amount of light into this oppressing, dark, and foul smelling pit of a room. The candles would also help to offset the stench of the place.

He pulled a small stool from one of the packs, unfolded it, and placed it near the cot, still not looking at the cot or the person on it. The stool was a three-legged folding stool that James had used for many years for hunting, and it was very sturdy. He placed the ice chest near the stool and set his Bible on the ice chest. A portable tape recorder, a large box of blank cassettes, and a large amount of batteries for the recorder were strategically placed to record the events that would take place in the hut. James kept his back turned to the cot as he surveyed the room and decided that it was as well-prepared as it could be. Going back outside, he instructed those gathered to rest, eat, and stay in an attitude of prayer, and that he would be back in a while. A number of local Pastors from the area along the main highway had heard of the events that were to happen and they also showed up on the remote mountain. They came to watch, and to offer assistance if they were able, but they were there mostly due to their curiosity. It had been a long overnight ride for those who came from the States, and they needed to rest and eat. As James was walking out into the yard, the family expressed their fears of him leaving with the door to the hut open. Two strong looking young men were appointed to be watchmen. This action seemed to calm some of the fears of the family and other onlookers.

James climbed up the side of Jefe Mountain to where a large boulder protruded out over the valley below. He sat on the boulder and looked out over the valley at the blue-green color of the distant floor of trees and other vegetation. It was quiet there, and outstandingly beautiful. The valley, about four thousand feet below, and the magnificent cliffs of the mountains on the other side of the valley, were beyond description. This rock would become a regular place of meditation and prayer for him, a place of solitude and retreat. Today it was a staging area for the battle that was about to be fought over this young woman's life and soul. As he prayed, he sought for God to guide him in every step that he was about to take. He told God that, on his own, he was already defeated and that if it was up to the abilities that he had, there was no need in starting to attempt to free this captive child. He pleaded with God to have His Spirit show the way, asking for the help of Angels, for the blood of Jesus to protect him and his family, and for everything he did to be ordained by God through the ministry of the Holy Spirit. James wept, not out of fear, but out of humility, knowing that through his weakness God would show strength.

Closing his prayer, he stated, "God, I will give my all to have this child freed. If it is necessary, I will lay down my life in whatever form and all that I ask of You, God, is to please free this child and take care of my family."

James entered the area of the compound and chose his wife, Jose, a local evangelist, Pifas, a pastor from the area, and an older itinerate Evangelist (who was eighty-one years old from the Yucatan area of Mexico) to accompany him into the hut. The old Evangelist was named Joselio, and no one on the mountain knew him, as he had just shown up that morning and offered to help. James had taken an immediate liking to Joselio. During the deliverance, many people would appear in the room, staying as long as they could and then leaving as someone else would usually take their place. Joselio was the one exception. He would stay with James and Phyllis throughout the deliverance. Joselio and Phyllis would stand by, pray, and do as instructed for the entire time. As the small entourage entered that mud hut, the forces of evil were gathering in the mountains surrounding the village. They were summoned from all over that area of the mountains, with some from many hundreds of miles away. Somne Octe's underlings knew that they had had control of these mountains for thousands of years and they felt that nothing was going to come to pass that Somne Octe did not order. The group entered the hut and closed the door, which now had the small opening uncovered. It was 8:00 a.m. on a Friday morning.

During the previous month of fasting and prayer it had been revealed to James that the main mistake made on the previous visit was limiting the time spent with the girl. From his Bible studies during the fast, he now knew that the demons were aware of what was going on around them. This was evident as during the previous trip he had announced to his wife, and inadvertently to the demons, that two hours was all he had. He now believed that they just retreated and hung on knowing that their torture would soon be over. That was a mistake, and the mistake would not be repeated. James sat down on the stool and moved around to be comfortable. He had chosen this stool because it was very comfortable. He had spent many hours sitting on it while deer hunting. It had a back and arms and it did a good job of supporting his back and legs during long hours of hunting. He reached over to the ice chest, picked up his Bible placed it in his lap, he then retrieved a bottle of Mexican Coca Cola. The Mexican-made Coke was much stronger and had far more caffeine that it's American counterpart.

He opened the Coke, took a long drink, and then another, and said, "Demons, listen to what I am about to say."

Turning to his wife, James told her that if Sara was not free by the end of the planned four day stay, she was to take the vehicle and go back to Texas. She was to run the business and take care of whatever necessities might arise and to return in thirty days, bringing fresh supplies. If Sara was not free by that time, she was to repeat the same instructions over and over. This was to be repeated no matter how long it took. James then stated that he was not going to leave the room until this child was free of her demonic possession. He also had some in attendance hang a blanket in one corner of the room and placed a bucket there for his, Joselio's, and his wife's necessities. He restated to everyone and to no one in particular that he was there to stay. This proclamation greatly upset the forces of evil that were present in the room and inside of Sara, and they began to react to the situation.

What was being said there was quickly relayed throughout the area among all the demons. The principalities, powers, and dominions of evil in the area were already abuzz. As the messages were being relayed up the chain of command, Somne Octe was issuing orders of his own. One, such as Sara, that they had control of in this eighth sector, for which Somne Octe was responsible, had never been lost back to the other side. Many had come and tried to gain release of one or another of the captives of the forces of darkness, but never, not even once, had these lowly humans been successful. This time would be no different. The establishment of a few Evangelical churches in the eighth sector had been bad enough. Even though they were innocuous and posed no real threat to the evil kingdom, they were still a mark on the reputation of the leader, and this could not be.

Somne Octe put out the mandate to bring all the loose spirits from the eighth sector (those not presently residing in a human or animal body).

"Summon my demons whose specialty is in controlling the animal kingdom," he screamed. "Summon my demons whose specialty is in tempting these humans. Summon my demons whose specialty is manipulating the elements. Summon my demons whose specialty is confusing the mind of these lowlife humans. Do it now! Do it now! We will put a stop to this here and now. Summon my demons whose specialty is sexual deviation. Do it now! We will give this fool, James, who has tried to invade our area, room to hang himself, become discouraged, and leave, but, just in case, I want the full force of my principality to be ready. Then, after this American is defeated here on this mountain, I will want him destroyed completely. I have never suffered a loss and neither will I this day."

Xanateo and his witches were privy to these communications and they also started trekking toward the mountain village. If something unspeakable were to take place with one they had trained, it would literally be hell for them to pay. They made their way and set up camp on the high part of the mountain above the village where they could observe the activities below.

Taking another drink of Coke and then setting the bottle on the floor, James looked down at Sara. She was the same as when he had left one month earlier. With pale skin, filthy matted hair, and puffy, swollen cheeks from the forced feeding, she was just as he had left her. Her grimy hands, with their three inch fingernails, were clasped around her own neck and she was breathing very shallowly. With the added light of the candles to accent the shaft of light coming through the hole that was now in the door, it was much easier to survey the room and the contents of that room. It did not take long to survey the contents: one roughly handmade small bed, one horsehair blanket, and some small dolls that seemed out of place. Upon close examination, the dolls were found to be curse dolls (similar to Voodoo dolls) with long, sharp splinters shoved through them. Later, James learned that the family members had prepared them. The family was ashamed of Sara and what had taken place, and Sara's father had made the dolls to try to end the embarrassment. The dolls had been thrown through the small opening of the door before it had been covered. They were an attempt to put the curse of death on Sara. The dolls were scattered around the floor by the door. They were gathered up, passed to the outside, and it was ordered that they be burned.

Sara was still covered with the filthy handmade horsehair cover. The cover was loosely woven and gave very little protection from the cold nights. It covered her from her armpits down to above her ankles. She was still obviously naked beneath the cover and her ankles and feet still seemed strangely clean. The smell of stale urine was still the most unbearable. The bed did not have a mattress but instead had a woven grass rope that had been woven back and forth across the rails of the bed. It was very rough and abrasive, and obviously soaked with stale urine, but the fecal smell that should have been there wasn't. As James sat and contemplated the whole of the situation, he saw some movement at the lower end of the bed. At first he thought it might be her feet, but when he looked through the near darkness in that direction, he saw two small mice, one going under the cover and one coming out. With a gut-wrenching realization, he knew why there was not a strong fecal odor. The mice were going under the covers and eating the fecal material off Sara's body. They were also licking and eating any dropped parts or smears from her legs and feet.

That is why that area of her body was clean and the rest wasn't. James fought off the nausea that came over him and thought, "Dear God, dear God, oh, dear God."

Reaching down and pulling one of her hands away from her throat, he pulled his folding knife out of the belt holster and cut off the three-inch nails. The thought crossed his mind that this was the same knife he had used on his boot the day the Angel came. He did the same to the other hand. It was not an easy task as the grip she had on her throat was surprisingly strong. He did this as a safety precaution, not for himself, but for the child. The nails seemed to be as dangerous as any weapon and he was concerned she might stab or cut herself with them. On the trip last month she had exhibited self-destructive tendencies and James fully expected them again. He kept trying to convince himself that no harm could come to him during this exorcism. He hoped that as long as he was doing the work of the Lord he would be protected, but he was in totally unfamiliar territory and had no idea of the harm that might befall him or his wife.

James started to pray. "Father God, in the name of your Holy Child Jesus, I believe I have the right to seek the freedom of this child. I do perceive her to be possessed by evil spirits. I know from your word that each time someone was delivered from evil spirits that they came seeking to be free, with the exceptions of when a family member came asking for them. This child's aunt, her caretaker, the one who has kept her alive, has asked me to pray for her deliverance. I believe, based on this, that I have the right, the authority from you through Christ and ministered by the Holy Spirit, to seek the deliverance of this child called Sara. Father, I ask that your Holy Spirit guide me and give me the words to say as is promised in the book of Acts in your Holy Scripture. Help me Father, for I am nothing without You."

He continued praying in a similar manner for the better part of an hour.

"You demons that are in Sara, I command you to leave her now! By the name of Christ Jesus of Nazareth I command you to leave! By the blood of Jesus Christ I say leave her now!" James spoke firmly.

Over and over and over he commanded the demons to leave Sara; over and over and over he invoked the name Jesus to try and force the demons to flee their warm and comfortable home.

"John fourteen – twelve, Jesus said that the works that He did the believer will also do and even greater works shall they do," he paraphrased from fourteenth chapter of John.

James repeatedly quoted this and other scriptures that gave believers the power to command demons to flee in the name of Jesus. There was no reaction from Sara, none whatsoever. In the spiritual world, all the forces of evil in that area waited and planned. They waited for this human to tire of his fanciful game and planned what they were going to do to him and his family. This intrusion into their domain would not be without cost. The demon Baltar, who had sent an underling to the United States to discourage the Americans from coming back to these mountains, was an expert at controlling human thought. He began sending some of those under his command to those who were beginning to gather on the side of the mountain. It was becoming a rather large group of inquisitive mountain folks gathering for the spectacle.

"Confuse them," he commanded, "Make them believe that this man is not here to help, but rather to bring misery to this one called Sara and everyone else who lives on the mountain."

Baltar also sent many of the evil hoards to the United States to bring about lies and gossip concerning this man of God.

"When he tires of this game, if he lives, when he returns home to the United States he will receive an onslaught of attacks from his fellow so-called believers," Baltar reported to Somne Octe.

Somne Octe stated, "Yes, we will teach these humans a great lesson. Steal all that he has, destroy the work he is trying to do, destroy his reputation, and then kill him and those with him, and do so in a way that is most repulsive to humans."

James spoke with full authority, "I command you demons, in the Name of Jesus Christ, to leave this child. By the authority of the Blood of Jesus Christ, I say to you to leave."

Again and again, the statement of authority and the commands were stated without a response from Sara. She lay perfectly still, breathing very softly. The demons were hanging on and resisting with all their power and with the encouragement of their superiors. Hours passed and the sun went down. The moon rose then set. The dawn was beginning to break. It was 6 a.m. on Saturday morning.

On the side of the mountain, nearly five hundred people had gathered to see what was going on. People throughout the whole area knew of Sara. As the word spread people began to come from their own villages or ranches to San Mateo. These were not necessarily good or evil souls, just curious people. They brought with them their food, horsehair blankets, and gourds filled with water. If something was going to happen, they wanted to see it. Inside of the hut it was the same: James praying and commanding, and Sara lying there. There was nothing for the people to see because nothing was happening. Nothing was happening in the visible world, but in the spiritual realm it was a different situation.

Twenty-three hours into the deliverance, the sun had been up for a while, but inside the hut it was nearly impossible to tell. James had taken his watch off at the beginning of the deliverance, not wanting to be distracted by the time. He then took a long drink of water out of a gourd that had been handed in through the small opening of the door. His body was telling him to quit. His mind was telling him to quit. The people who came with him were telling him to quit. The family of Sara was telling him to quit. The indigenous Pastors and Evangelists were telling him to quit, except the old man, Joselio, who was encouraging him to go on. James' heart was telling him to continue. His wife put her arm around his tired shoulders, told him to do as God instructed, and assured him that she was right there beside him, no matter what.

Chapter 17

When James had finished the gourd of water, he sat back down on the stool by Sara, and prayed. "God, your word says in the book of Acts that I am not to be concerned about the words to say, for your Holy Spirit will give them to me. I believe this with all my heart and I now ask for those words. Your Word also states in the book of James that if I want wisdom, all I have to do is ask and you will give it to me liberally. Well, I'm asking."

He then leaned over the young girl, opened his mouth, and sternly commanded, "You foul demon, you fallen angel, you of whatever principality, or power, or dominion, I say to you to respond to this command. Who are you? Why are you here? Show yourself, I command you by all that is Holy. I command this in the name of all names, the name of Jesus Christ, Son of the Almighty God."

James felt all the fatigue leave his body and mind, and then strength and a power rose up within the core of his very being.

He responded to this by saying, "Now, I command you, in the Name of Jesus, now!"

Sara's body began to stir and her mouth opened. She appeared about to speak when her hands clenched down on her throat.

She began making gurgling sounds and everyone that was in the room realized she was truly choking herself. James reached forward and grabbed her by the wrist to pull her hands away. He was a large and strong man but he could not clear her hands from the choking grip she had on herself. Sara's eyes opened and rolled back in her head. Her chest was heaving for air and there was a small trickle of blood coming out of the corner of her mouth.

"Release her by all that is Holy, by the blood of Christ, release her!" James grabbed her wrist again and pulled so hard that he was concerned that her wrist would break. "God, Please" he begged.

Her grip came loose and she fell back on the bed.

She then rose up on one elbow turned toward James and his wife and said, "You (expletive deleted), you stupid weak (expletive deleted) humans."

Her voice was as a man's voice, deep, raspy, loud and speaking in English with the same Cajun accent as before, "Do you think you can order me with puny names of defeated ones? Do you think that using the name of one defeated by my King, one killed by Lucifer, will avail anything? This Jesus that you call on is defeated and dead and gone. Now you leave me to my work. Go! Go! Go!"

Sara was now sitting up in the bed. Really dark bruises were on her throat and the blood still ran down her face. Her cover had fallen away, exposing her nakedness, but she paid it no attention. Her mouth was moving, but her eyes were as blank and lifeless as a body on an autopsy table. James noticed the dark pentagram scar on the girl's chest between her breast, and wondered where that might have come from, and what the story behind it was.

Phyllis came close and reached to cover Sara's nakedness but the voice screamed, "Don't touch me you bitch! Leave me alone! I will show my (expletive deleted) to whomever I want to show it to."

Phyllis realized that the demon was just trying to set a diversion, and she stepped back, deciding to cover her later and to not let the demon get them distracted.

James was leaning over and looking straight into Sara's deathly eyes. "I order you, evil spirit, to tell me who you are. Tell me now."

Sara spoke again in the man's voice, "I told you that you cannot order me to do or say anything. You frail, stupid, miserable and mislead human. You lose, you are defeated."

Sara's body began to convulse and large knots the size of a man's fist came up on her slim stomach. "I am Basar, and this piece of miserable human flesh is mine to live in and to destroy as I see fit. My underlings and I are here with authority and you have no power over us, and cannot order us to do anything."

Sara fell down on the cot and her body jerked and twisted; the knots (the knots resembled really large muscle spasms) appeared over her whole body. She began to cry, scream, and beg the Americans.

This time she used a little girl's voice and spoke in Spanish. "Help me! You are killing me! Please leave me alone, you are killing me! I never did anything to you, why are you hurting me?"

She then fell limp on the bed and her hands went back to the previous position around her throat, clasping but not choking herself. The girl was absolutely motionless. Phyllis came close to the cot, covered Sara, brushed her hair back out of her face and cleaned off as much of the blood as she could. It was now approximately 8:30 a.m. Saturday morning.

James sat still for a moment and then informed the other Pastors who had rotated into the room to give a break to the others for a while, a synopsis of what had taken place. As he sat there, he retrieved a fresh Coke and a protein bar and contemplated what had really just taken place. The demon had responded and did what was commanded of him. Now the evil spirit had fussed, fought, complained, delayed and obfuscated, but he had also stated what his name was, where he was, and what he was doing. He had succumbed, at least up to a point, to the power of the name of the Lord Jesus. Now James had read many books and heard many sermons and lectures on deliverance. None of them said it might take 23 or 24 hours for a demon to respond, and just to respond and not vacate the possessed person. They all had said to simply speak the name of Jesus and all demons would have to flee. One man had the audacity to state that he was such a Godly man and so full of the Holy Ghost that all he had to do was walk in a room and all the demons would run over themselves to flee. This just did not live up to the Scripture, and certainly did not line up with last 24 hours. James recalled that during the previous month of fasting and prayer, as he had read over the scriptures about Jesus casting out demons, he had learned a lot. He had quit reading in the light of all those claims he had heard over the years, and searched for what the scriptures really said.

The revelation was amazing. He recalled a passage of scripture in the gospel of Mark that he had memorized concerning setting the captives free.

Mark 5:1:

"And they came over unto the other side of the sea, into the country of the Gadarenes. And when he was come out of the ship, immediately there met him out of the tombs a man with an unclean spirit, Who had his dwelling among the tombs; and no man could bind him, no, not with chains: Because that he had been often bound with fetters and chains, and the chains had been plucked asunder by him, and the fetters broken in pieces: neither could any man tame him. And always, night and day, he was in the mountains, and in the tombs, crying, and cutting himself with stones. But when he saw Jesus afar off, he ran and worshipped him, And cried with a loud voice, and said, what have I to do with thee, Jesus, thou Son of the most high God? I adjure thee by God, that thou torment me not. For he said unto him, Come out of the man, thou unclean spirit. And he asked him, What is thy name? And he answered, saying, My name is Legion: for we are many. And he besought him much (argued with him much) that he would not send them away out of the country. Now there was there nigh unto the mountains a great herd of swine feeding. And all the devils besought him (argued with him)…"

Whether there were six thousand evil spirits or six hundred, James did not know. He did know that there were many, and they argued with the Son of God, the Deliverer of mankind. Scripture does not state specifically how long it took for the arguing to take place, but it did take time for "much arguing" to pass, very possibly a lot of time. The process of delivering the demonic of the tombs, as related in the above paragraph was not an instant occurrence, but rather a process, even for Jesus Christ Himself. The Holy Spirit had brought much confidence to James by bringing the understanding of these and other scriptures to his remembrance.

By hour twenty-seven, approximately another hundred locals had gathered. Now there were an estimated six hundred men, women, and children watching the compound that contained the mud hut where the exorcism was taking place. They were a few hundred yards away, but they were sill watching. Word had quickly spread that Sara had spoke, and the buzz was that maybe there was something good about to happen. Maybe, just maybe, these Hallelujahs (as Christians were called by the locals) were not such a bad thing after all. As the families gathered on the side of the mountain, the men visited, the women went about the duties of caring for the families, and the children played. On the other side of Jefe Mountain, something far more sinister was taking place.

On the other side of "El Jefe," the demonic forces were at work, and the ravens called "Negros Grandes" (big blacks) were gathering. It was not unusual for them to be in large flocks, but this gathering was larger than anyone's recollection or imagination. Tens of thousands of extremely large ravens assembled together and started flying over the mountains. They flew around the 13,000 foot peak of Jefe Mountain in the passes that were a few thousand feet lower in altitude than the peak. Then the massive flock came to the sloping meadows overlooking San Mateo, the meadows where the curious were gathered. The ravens came swooping down to the ground. At first they were only picking at the food the families had brought, but then they started to fly into and peck at the people themselves. The birds harassing the people of the mountains were not an uncommon occurrence, but there was something decidedly different about the birds this day. The first birds caused some concern and discomfort to those gathered, but as more and more of the large black birds came down, discomfort turned to pandemonium. The women were screaming and trying to protect their children. The men were swinging sticks and machetes at the birds and hitting other people as often as they were hitting the birds. Total panic engulfed the six hundred or so people on the side of the mountain.

Jezel, one of the demons with the power to control animals, watched as his handywork totally decimated the gathering of curious onlookers. Somne Octe was pleased and ordered Fenet to use his expertise, which is that of bringing confusion, to confuse the people about what was happening.

"Fenet, go and convince the weak, frightened humans that this danger is upon them because of the presence of those with Sara," Somne Octe boomed.

Fenet and his minions went and did as instructed. The confused people began to believe that James and his companions were causing them to be attacked by the hoard of birds. As they ran and tried to take cover, they screamed at each other that this gringo, this American missionary and all the Christians had to leave or all the people in the village would die.

When the report came to James of what was taking place, he told the indigenous Pastors and Evangelist to go and stand among the people and show no fear, for harm would not come to them. He believed this might restore some sense of order and that the demonic attack would cease. The men went out of the compound carrying their Bibles and praying. The birds did not attack them, but Fenet had his underlings plant the idea in the minds of the locals that these men were controlling the birds. It was an easy confusion to bring, for the Believers were not being attacked. The birds left after an hour, but the newly found hatred of the Christians, and especially the hatred for the Americans, remained and permeated the group. As they gathered, they spoke much evil and placed many bad omens and curses on what was taking place in the mud hut they were observing.

It was now hour thirty and James had refused to be distracted by the noise and confusion surrounding the hut where he, his wife, Joselio, and two other Believers continued praying for Sara.

"Come out of her you foul demon, I command you to come out of her now, in the name of Jesus and by the authority I have as a Believer. Come out of her, release her, set her free!" James stood by his belief in what the scriptures had said.

Chapter 18

Fatigue had set in again a few hours earlier but now it was as if he had had eight hours of solid sleep, though of course neither Phyllis nor he had had any. The locals that rotated being in the hut had the opportunity for some rest, but James was determined not to stop or even slow down. Phyllis was just as determined to stand by her husband throughout this ordeal, whatever it took, wherever it went. Sara stirred on the filthy cot. It had been a while since she had even moved. The only movement recently was when Phyllis tried to dress her. The aunt had brought Sara's baptism dress to the hut. They wanted her to be covered as she had brought enough embarrassment on them as it was. Strange as it seemed, the immediate family was much more concerned with their embarrassment than with their daughter's condition. Whenever Phyllis would approach Sara to dress her, she would be cussed at and screamed at in a man's voice speaking English.

James finally told his wife not to be concerned about that now. "When she is fully delivered, you can fix her up anyway you want."

Sara stirred again and her body arched upwards at the midsection and then slammed against the wall with a resounding thud. When she fell back on the cot, her body was again slammed against the wall. Joselio was praying as James and Phyllis reached for the girl to hold her on the bed, but when they touched her, she screamed at the top of her lungs.

In Spanish, in a little girl's voice, she screamed, "They are killing me, some of you help me! These gringos, these stupid Americans, these so called Hallelujahs are killing me. They are burning me. I am going to burn to death. Help me please. Make them quit, make them leave, stop them, please, please, please!"

Her voice was pleading and whimpering. Jim smelled the distinct odor of burning flesh and looked down at Sara. Burn marks appeared everywhere that he or his wife had touched on her body. Deep, red welts rose even more on the girls flesh as she continued her ranting and screaming.

James asked his wife to step back, and he commanded the demon, "By all that is Holy, and by every name that is named, I command you to cease. By the name of Jesus Christ of Nazareth, stop torturing this child and leave her now."

Without realizing it, his voice had risen in volume and was a booming force in the small hut.

Sara's body went limp and the demon spoke from her in English with the Cajun accent, "All right, all right, you win, I am leaving, you can have this sorry piece of human flesh, as I have had my fill of her."

The child's body began convulsing and the knots began to come up on her stomach, thighs and forearms. She began to cry and then scream and beg. Then there was a sound like no one in the hut, outside the hut, or on the side of the mountain had ever heard before. When it started, for some reason, the American thought about a banshee. Somewhere he had heard an old saying about screaming like a banshee. The door had been opened and one of the ravens had come inside the hut. It landed at the edge of the cot as those inside covered their ears. The sound that started from Sara seemed to move to the raven, and then began to come from the raven. Then the bird flew across the room, then outside and up the side of the mountain. The loud scream seeming to come from the bird was near deafening. Everyone in and around the village heard the sound leave the hut and disappear over the mountain.

Sara fell back on the bed and said in her childlike Spanish voice, "Gracia, gracia, muchas gracias." (Thank you, thank you, thanks very much) She smiled a sweet smile, tried to sit up the best she could, and repeated her thanks, "Gracias."

The local pastors in the hut started shouting and as the word spread outside, those present began to rejoice and shout that "Sara is free, Sara is free, the spirits have left; Sara is free!"

The onlookers on the side of the mountain heard and continued the chant. Sara is free, Sara is free. Everyone was rejoicing and shouting out loudly. The other locals in and around the hut tried to get James to come out and join them. Phyllis looked at her husband, and as he met her glance he slowly shook his head. His eyes were communicating one thing, but his spirit was saying something entirely different. Joselio nodded with knowing approval.

At hour thirty-two, James looked at the child. She appeared frail, with burn marks on her arms and shoulders and blood ran down from the side of her face from a cut on her forehead where she had hit the wall so many times. She was so innocent looking, with tears in her eyes, gratitude on her lips, and a slight smile.

James took a deep breath, downed some Coke, told his wife to move back a little, and spoke out, "You foul wretched lying demon, you messenger from hell, you fallen angel, I said I command you to leave her now, and I mean now! I will not fall for your games, your lies, or your diversions. By the blood of Jesus and by my authority as a Believer, you will do as you are commanded."

Sara's body stiffened and instantly she was standing on the cot. She did not get up; it was as though she was bounced off a trampoline. Though she was short, the low roof was touching her head as she stood with her feet about two feet apart, her fists clenched, and her eyes were absolutely totally bloodshot, the eyes also seemed to glow. Her nostrils were flared, perspiration started pouring from her skin, and her upper lip curled up as she began to shudder from her head all the way down to her feet.

She leaned forward so that her face was about six inches from James' face, and the demon spoke in English, this time with a British accent, "You will die this day; we will string your guts from the fence posts for the birds to eat. We will rape your wife and when we are through with her we will throw her wretched body to the pigs for them to feast on as she screams and begs in futility. You have earned the total wrath of Somne Octe and you will pay."

The girl's eyes seemed to glow brighter and brighter in the dim, candle-lit room. She began cursing more than any sailor on a drunken binge. She also started spitting at the couple and acting as though she was going to scratch or hit them. As she continued to scream and curse, her eyes glowed brighter, and everything in the room began to vibrate and shake. The candles went out, the half empty Coke bottle flew across the room, and the Coleman lantern turned over; thankfully it had not yet been lit. The room was in chaos, but James, Phyllis, and Joselio knew to continue praying.

Some of the curious crowd in the yard next to the hut looked inside. The door, at this time, was partly ajar and the small window also afforded some opportunity to peek inside. What they saw sent them quickly away in an absolute panic. Sara was totally naked, standing on the cot, and her eyes were like red-beamed flashlights. Foam and what seemed to be smoke came out of her mouth in copious amounts. Many of the faithful on the outside quickly became unfaithful, full of fear and terror. They ran down the mountain screaming and telling everyone what they had witnessed. The recipients of the news also were overcome by fear and ran. Terror ran rampant across the mountain like a wild fire on a prairie. More than half of the onlookers on the mountain quickly took their leave and went home to board themselves inside. Their fear turned to anger at the American doing the exorcism. The talk was to run these people off the mountain, but no one had the courage to approach the hut. Their fearful minds became fertile ground for the demons to plant more confusion and lies. They believed that the red-eyed monster from the hut had murdered dozens and dozens of their fellow villagers. They remembered when Sara had burned her parents' hut and tried to kill her whole family. They knew that their huts would be next. They all began to smell smoke and hear screams that were not there, at least not yet.

Living up to one of the titles given to Lucifer in the New Testament, "Prince of the Power of the Air," the evil forces caused a small and very black cloud to form around the top of Jefe Mountain. It was not unusual for weather to form on the top of the mountains, but not this time of year and certainly not this rapidly. A sirocco wind began to blow from the south and the cloud approached from the north. A sirocco wind is a hot, dry, extremely hard wind stirred by the heat on the desert below the mountains. This was not the time of year for this to happen. A storm cloud wasn't supposed to be there, and the sirocco wind wasn't supposed to be there, but there they were none the less. Somne Octe had ordered his minions to unleash everything possible against the travesty that was taking place. He knew his demons were getting weak in the battle going on in the hut and this could not be permitted. He could not lose this battle, for he knew that it was not just a battle for the pathetic little girl, but for his rule over this area. If he lost this battle in front of this many witnesses, his fate would not bid well with his master.

"Go! Go!" He commanded his many thousands of demons. "Go and release fear and terror and hatred among them! Go and twist the minds of all those of the mountain! Turn loose the elements, storms, hail, and lighting! Go and shake the earth! Go and turn the animals against the humans! Go! Go! Go! Set perverse thoughts in the minds of all. Whatever you do, you stop this so called messenger, this one called James. Stop the Hallelujah; destroy him and his wife and the girl. Do it now. Go! Go! Go!"

On the side of the mountain an eerie calm descended on everyone and everything. The sirocco wind went calm. The terrifying cloud stopped increasing and stood still in the sky. The animals calmed. The people's fear began to subside. In the mud hut, Sara lay down and allowed Phyllis to cover her but not to clothe her. The three local Pastors who had overcome their terror stood outside the hut's door, relaxed and talked of victory. The few faithful left outside of the hut began to sing, laugh, and talk. The families who remained on the side of the mountain were fixing food and talking among each other. It was as though this place had turned from hell on earth to "Rebecca of Sunnybrook Farm." In his spirit, James knew better. He hugged and comforted his wife and told her to rise above what was going to happen.

"Remember," he told his wife, "We can do all things through Christ Jesus who gives us strength. We win, Phyllis. I've read the last page in the Book. WE WIN!"

James encouraged himself not to be swayed by what they might see, feel or hear. God had spoken to his heart again and this was a battle for the hearts and souls of these wonderful people in these mountains, and James knew they were going to prevail, through the Name of Jesus. Whatever it took, they were going to prevail.

He spoke quietly and sincerely, "What might or might not happen to us is of little consequence compared to what will happen to these people if we quit and walk away."

Phyllis nodded in agreement and they stood up in the foul smelling, demon filled place, consoling each other and praying for courage, wisdom, and guidance.

The dry, hot blast of south wind blew through the village at close to eighty miles per hour. It scattered everything that was not tied down and even some things that were. There was no warning, just calm, then chaos. The few children that were outside were blown around by the horrific wind. Chickens were picked up in the air and joining clothes, buckets, and other small items that were blown to who knows were. The hut, were Sara was, shook when the wind blasted against its side and roof. Inside, Jim was not surprised by this, or actually anything else that might take place. Many Bible scholars and teachers would tell you that the demons only mess with your mind. They taught that the demons, if they exist, could not do anything physical. He had heard this all his life, but he preferred to believe what the Bible said, and not these so-called religious teachers. In the Book of Peter, Satan is described as seeking whom he may destroy and kill. In the book of Ephesians, Satan is referred to as the "Prince of the power of the air" and in another place the earth is designated as the "kingdom of Satan." James had come to the irrefutable conclusion that Satan can do what he wishes through his minions on the earth. True Believers in Jesus Christ are the only exception. Those who have the indwelling of the Holy Spirit and faith in what the Word says have protection from this enemy, but even they must believe this and act on it. The non-believer and the elements are fair game. This is what this man had learned from fasting and studying the Holy Scriptures and those Scriptures from which he drew his faith. He and his wife stood on that belief as all hell began breaking out around them.

The wind was howling as loud as a train-whistle outside the hut. The roof of the hut was shaking and on the verge of coming off. Sticks, small logs, chickens, buckets and other items were hitting and bouncing off the outside wall. Inside, James continued to pray for Sara, continuing to order the demons to leave and not do her any more harm. Phyllis was doing as her husband had instructed her and was taking authority over those demons controlling the elements. She was walking around the room, praying and commanding the demons not to destroy the hut. The door had been blown open and was impossible to pull back into place. Dust and other elements filled the air in the hut, making it nearly impossible to see and difficult to breathe. The demons in Sara were responding to the onslaught of prayer and commands. The demons in full "besought Him much mode" as related in the story of the demoniac in the tombs. The demons were arguing profusely with James

They argued with everything that was said to them. There were so many different voices and accents and languages coming from Sara that trying to keep track of them was futile. Even later, listening to the tape recordings of the deliverance, it was nearly impossible to separate all the different voices. James was staying with what he believed, and not responding to their arguments, he just stated his authority and commanded them to leave and stop hurting the girl. He had some major concerns about the girl's physical well being. She was cut, bruised, bleeding, and the nearly constant knotting of her muscles had to be doing damage.

James had read in many modern "Deliverance" books that all a person had to do was to say, "Come out in the name of Jesus and do not hurt the person," and the demon could not bring harm. James thought, "What planet do these people come from?" In his month of fasting and prayer, he had memorized many scriptures, and many of these spoke of the demons doing harm.

One of these was the passage in the Book of Mark. In the ninth chapter is the story of the boy with an evil spirit. In the twenty-fifth verse *"When Jesus saw that the people came running together, He rebuked the foul spirit. Saying unto him, "thou dumb and deaf spirit, I charge thee, come out of him, and enter no more into him." And the spirit cried and tore the boy sore and came out of him: and the boy was as though dead."* This was

Jesus, Son of God, Savior of all mankind; and the demon tore the boy so bad everyone thought the boy was dead. James had decided that with all the misinformation abound in the books and teachings on deliverance, the authors and teachers had never read the scriptures.

"What in the world were those teachers of deliverances thinking?" James wondered. "How much pain had their wrong writings and false teaching caused? How many sincere believers had gotten discouraged when things had not worked out the way these people had said that it would? How many possessed souls had remained that way because of these false teachings?"

"Dear God," James prayed, "help us all to learn the scriptures."

A child's voice was now speaking out of Sara in Spanish. She was addressing the native Pastors and trying to convince them that she was all right and that this American was going to kill her. If she died, the fault would be laid at their feet and God would reject them. Most of the indigenous ministers were by now fearful of the whole situation, but where could they go? If they went outside they would certainly be harmed in the sirocco wind. The danger of the debris flying about in the ferocious wind was real and urgent. The senior member of the group, the eighty-something-year-old from the Yucatan, chastised the others for their fear, telling them to continue to pray or to get off the mountain. When the demons saw that the local Pastors were not going to interfere, a new tactic was tried. Sara pulled back the covers to expose her naked body again and this time addressed James by a nickname that he had had when he was in Vietnam

Sara was speaking with an oriental accent that reminded James of the street prostitutes in Vietnam, those that he had encountered in Saigon. "Hey Kahuna, I make you feel very very good American GI. I do anything. I do everything. You know you want good time, I give you good time. Come on over here, you, hey you, Big Kahuna, you come here."

James was quite shaken by this turn of events. The guys in his outfit in Vietnam had called him the Big Kahuna many years before, and he had never used that name again; even his wife did not know about it. He had never expected anything like this. How in the world did the demons know a nickname from twelve years before and halfway around the world? He made a mental note to learn more about this principality, powers, and dominion thing, then quickly came back to the situation.

His voice showed dogged determination as he spoke to the demon. "Cease you foul spirit, cease and desist and come out of her."

Sara fell back on the cot and said with a May West accent, "Hey big boy, can't a girl have a little fun?"

The depth of knowledge of these demons and the myriad of antics astounded James but he didn't think about it long, for there was a loud boom that shook the hut so severely that dust rained down from the mud bricks and the thatch roof.

The deliverance had been going on for thirty-six hours when the dry, hot sirocco winds that had blown up the mountain collided with the cool, wet, black clouds; nature was taking its course. The friction of the two widely disparaging winds built up a massive amount of static electricity. The black cloud was now massive in size, probably 40,000 ft. high and it was quickly moving over San Mateo. The tremendous boom of a bolt of lighting again shook the hut and the rest of the village. This was just the beginning. Large hailstones began to fall and pile up on the ground; as the cloud moved over San Mateo, a virtual torrent of lighting bolts was unleashed, striking the ground, the huts and some of the animals. Over and over, millions of volts of electricity were released as the blinding flashes delivered their destruction. Many fires were started, some of huts, some of outbuildings, and many in the grass. The hut where the deliverance was taking place was barely missed by a massive bolt. It set fire to some animal fodder and the fire quickly spread to the thatch roof of the hut.

As the thatch started to burn, one of the demons spoke out, "You can stop this and save the village, you can be a hero. Just leave this room and peace will return. What is this girl compared to the destruction of the whole village?"

James instructed those in attendance to seek God for deliverance of the village, to petition Father God in the name of Jesus for this destruction to cease. Two local Pastors, Joselio, Phyllis, and James prostrated themselves on the filthy floor and begged God for deliverance. The fire went out after consuming about one third of the roof. The booming ceased almost immediately. The clouds dispersed and the people started coming out of the huts to survey the damage. The demons had not been able to destroy the village, but they were hard at work putting blame for this on the events taking place in the hut.

It had been thirty-eight hours into the deliverance when Phyllis heard the barking of the first dog. More of a barking growl than just a bark, it was the kind of sound made when dogs are fighting each other. One of the demons in Sara spoke to those in the hut and said that their time would be short, for they would be destroyed and eaten by the dogs. Every dog in the village and the surrounding area began running towards the top of the rise where the deliverance was taking place. There were hundreds of large, strong mountain lion and bear-killing dogs coming to the hut. The residents were trying to keep their own dogs at home but it was to no avail. All the dogs were fighting each other, foaming at the mouth, and completely intent on surrounding the small mud hut.

At the same time, all the other animals on the mountain went absolutely berserk. Horses, mules, donkeys, chickens, pigs, goats, sheep – none were immune to the madness that swept across the village and surrounding area. At the compound where the hut was situated, a large mule had broken its tether and was kicking at anything that it could. The main object of the mule's wrath was the rickety door on the hut. It was kicked over and over until it was totally destroyed and the large rope hinges were torn apart. The mule then vented its anger on the fences and other objects in the compound before running at full speed down the mountain. The attack of the mule might seem random to an observer, but not to Somne Octe and his minions, who were coordinating the animal attacks. Somne Octe was pleased when he saw that the door was now gone from the hut and those worthless humans would have no way of escaping the hoards of angry, crazed dogs.

At the same time, the dogs had gotten really close, and Sara was again being flung against the wall. This time she was flung with more force and violence than before. James told Phyllis to get by the door and pray as she had never prayed before.

Phyllis got to the door at the same time as the first of the dogs. She knelt down just inside the open doorway and sought God for protection. James grabbed Sara, ignoring her complaints of burning and forced her on the cot. He covered her with the cover so his flesh might not burn hers and placed his knee on her mid-section to hold her down. He was hoping that this might keep her from being severely injured. In the doorway, eight or ten of the dogs were barking, growling, and trying to lunge into the hut to get to Phyllis and the others. But they could not! The doorway was open and the dogs' foaming, growling mouths were within inches of Phyllis's face, but they seemingly could not come closer. They tried and tried, and lunged and growled, and barked and bit each other, but they were barred from entering the hut by an unseen Spiritual force. Sara somehow slid out from under Jim's knee and stood on the cot again.

Cursing and spitting, and speaking in many voices, she finally looked toward Phyllis and screamed, "Hey, Phyllis, you bitch, look over here!"

Phyllis lost her concentration for a moment and looked at the poor, wretched girl. As she did, Sara, without moving her lower torso, twisted her upper body and contorted herself to where Phyllis could see the shoulder blades. She then continued twisting her head until she was completely contorted and facing Phyllis.

Sara then screamed, "How about that, you (expletive deleted) bitch?!"

While this most extraordinary display was distracting Phyllis, one of the dogs came through the opening left by the mule kicked broken door. The crazed animal ignored Phyllis, but headed for her husband. The old Evangelist from the Yucatan pulled out his "machete" and struck the menacing dog in the back of the neck before he could do any harm. The blow with the sharp weapon nearly decapitated the animal and the dog immediately fell dead. Everyone in these mountains carried one of these long-bladed instruments, Pastors and farmers alike. The old man smiled and said that sometimes it is necessary to help prayers along. Phyllis ignored the distraction of Sara's contorted, naked, and bleeding body and went back to praying and protecting the door. Phyllis had been warned by her husband that she might see many things that looked impossible, and that what she would see was probably only the demons trying to distract and cause fear. She had been told to ignore whatever came and whatever she saw, but with Sara's body seemingly twisted like a pretzel, ignoring that sight was most difficult to accomplish. Sara's body went back to normal, but the ranting and raving continued. There were probably close to ninety dogs around the mud hut. They were digging and trying to get through the walls and some of them had their mouths stuck into the room through the holes they had dug. This had been going on for more than an hour when James decided enough was enough. He got prostrate on the floor and sought God for direction.

What he received was a scripture from the eighth chapter of Romans, the twenty-sixth verse: "*Likewise the Spirit also helps in our weaknesses. For we do not know what we should pray for as we should, but the Spirit Himself makes intercession for us with groanings which cannot be uttered.*" James stood and gave his total being over to the Spirit of God that resided in him.

"Ord di be son de lija ba deio. Sonta diati okse bataleo Christos," he proclaimed at the top of his voice, having not a clue what was being said.

Silence immediately engulfed the area. The dogs left. The other animals were calmed. Sara lay down and covered herself. The two local Pastors immediately vacated the premises, leaving only James, Phyllis, and the old man, Joselio, to continue.

James walked over to his wife, helped her up, dusted her off, hugged her, and with a deep sigh and a slight smile said, "Hey Toto, I don't think we're in Kansas anymore"

Chapter 19

Thirty nine hours had passed when Somne Octe was having what could best be described as a screaming hissy fit. He berated his minions for their weakness, demoted many of them, punished others in many perverse ways, and banished others to the dry places in the desert or the remote mountains.

He was screaming loudly, ranting and raving, finally saying, "If you cannot handle this I will go and do it myself."

Many of the demons argued with him, telling him it is beneath his position to do what he was planning. After all he was third in command with only Damion and Lucifer himself above him in this particular hierarchy.

Somne Octe responded, "You fools, I have been informed that Damion and our supreme leader, the Prince himself, Lucifer, will be here shortly. This situation must be dealt with and dealt with now."

Upon hearing this, the demons were struck with fear: Damien and Lucifer here, together? Heads would roll if things were not fixed and this American human discredited, destroyed and dead. Somne Octe slipped quietly into the hut and into Sara's body. It felt so good to have a body to be in; sometimes administration did have its downfalls. Now to deal with this arrogant, puny excuse of a human, the American would be running in no time. When he did run, his faith would be down and he would be vulnerable to a death of the most interesting kind.

James requested that his wife pray over Sara while he sought God for more instructions. He went to the backside of the room, prostrated himself and went into deep sincere communion with God. Joselio stood by Phyllis as she started taking authority over the demons. Joselio's part was to support and to pray for protection over Phyllis. As James got deeper into prayer, the irony of the fact that there were only three left was not lost on him. A relatively inexperienced preacher, his wife, and an aged, decrepit traveling preacher were all that was left. At that stage James felt that the aged preacher might have left if he weren't so feeble, but he later realized the resilience of Joselio. There was also irony in the fact that none of them had any great experience in deliverances. Yes, James needed guidance and wisdom and he knew he was going to the right place to receive it.

Somne Octe was all over the demons residing in Sara, saying, "I told you to kill her, I, the leader of the eighth sector, ordered you and you disobeyed. You will pay dearly for your disobedience."

They answered that they had tried, but had been blocked by the authority and prayers of that American human.

Somne Octe ranted back, "How many of these bible-toting, self-elevating, wretched and pathetic professed believers have we stripped naked and ran out of our mountains? No one can stand against us. I will show you and then you will pay more than you ever thought possible."

Forty hours had passed when James replaced his wife at the cot where Sara had resumed her normal position, with her body stiff and her hands clasped around her neck. She was breathing so shallowly that one could hardly tell she was alive. James started praying in his prayer language and then everything took a turn, again. Sara sprang up and stood on the cot, leaned towards James, and began to scream in a completely different voice than she had exhibited before. The voice was so loud that James' ears began to ring and to become quite painful. Phyllis and Joselio covered their ears but for some reason James felt like it was better for him not to show discomfort at this particular time.

The voice from inside of Sara screamed, "I AM SOMNE OCTE, RULER OF THE EIGTH SECTOR, YOU ARE TRESPASSING ON MY TERRITORY. YOU ARE ATTEMPTING TO STEAL MY POSSESSION AND YOU WILL NOT BE TOLERATED! MY AUTHORITY IS GIVEN BY THE PRINCE OF THE POWER OF THE AIR, BY THE GLORIOIUS ONE, LUCIFER HIMSELF. I TELL YOU TO LEAVE NOW OR DIE A HORRID DEATH YOU CANNOT EVEN IMAGINE. FEEL MY POWER, SUCCUMB TO MY AUTHORITY, RECOGNIZE WITH WHOM YOU ARE DEALING. I SHOW YOU NOW! NOW! NOW!"

Sara's body went horizontal, rose, and levitated a full two feet above the cot. She began to scream in her own voice as boils and lacerations appeared on her flesh. Her body began to shake as if a dog was using her as a chew toy. The temperature in the room dropped below zero. Everyone's breath was vaporizing as if on a snowy mountain in Colorado. Phyllis went to the door to see what kind of terrible weather had blown in. As she stood in the door, her back was freezing cold but her front facing the outside felt the warmth from outside. The temperature outside was the usual sixty degrees for this season of the year and for the time of night. The candles all blew out at the same time and the booming voice started again. The voice repeated the previous threats over and over.

James found a flashlight in the dark and got the Coleman lantern lit and immediately the lantern went out. At the same time the lantern went out, the candles relit by themselves. Then all the candles except the one by Joselio went out and did not relight. James was just on the verge of having the others leave, when the cold left and the room became unbearably hot. Sweat poured off of all in the room, and then the temperature went up and down and up and down. Zero to one hundred and twenty, one hundred and twenty to zero, zero to one hundred and twenty, over and over the temperature fluctuated. Sara's body was then nearly completely covered with bruises, burns, boils and lacerations.

The booming voice was now screaming, "YOU, PREACHER BOY, WATCH HER DIE, WATCH HER DIE A HORRIBLE DEATH THAT ONLY YOU CAN STOP. LEAVE NOW! ADMIT THAT LUCIFER IS THE GOD OF THIS PLACE. LEAVE NOW!"

Seeing what was happening to the girl drove James to the brink of desperation and maybe even closer to just flat-out and total despair. He took a deep breath and prayed silently for a few more moments.

He stopped praying, stood up, rolled his sleeves up above the elbows, opened his mouth and said, "I adjure you demon to cease your torture of this child. By every name that is holy, I command you to be obedient or I will bind you with chains here and now and hold you for your just punishment of everlasting fire. By the Name of Jesus Christ of Nazareth, by the Name of Adoni, by the name of the unspeakable Tetragrammaton, by the Name of Father God, Creator of all things, I command you to cease and desist. By the fires that create and destroy, I command you. Lucifer was created by Father God and will be destroyed by Father God. All things have been given unto His Son, Christ Jesus, and I command you with the authority given to me by the Blood of that self-same Christ Jesus. I say stop! Cease!"

James' fists were clenched and his face was flushed red in the pale light of the one candle. The veins were standing out on his neck and on his forehead. He grabbed Sara by the shoulders and pulled her face close to his.

He repeated the command will his voice full confidence and authority, "I adjure you demon to cease your torture of this child. By every name that is holy. I command you to be obedient or I will bind you with chains here and now and hold you for your just punishment of everlasting fire. By the Name of Jesus Christ of Nazareth, by the Name of Adoni, by the name of the unspeakable Tetragrammaton, by the Name of Father God, Creator of all things, I command you to cease and desist. By the fires that create and destroy, I command you. Lucifer was created by Father God and will be destroyed by Father God. All things have been given unto His Son, Christ Jesus, and I command you with the authority given to me by the Blood of that self-same Christ Jesus. I say stop! Cease!"

His eyes were not over two inches from Sara's when he screamed, "You want to fight Somne Octe? You want to see whose master is greatest? Listen to me, Somne Octe, ruler of the eighth sector. Let's do this! Here and now! Your turf or mine!"

Phyllis was staring at her husband in absolute disbelief. This whole thing that had been taking place was really more than strange, but this "your turf or mine," business frightened Phyllis. "Oh my God, please help him, please help us" she prayed silently.

Once again James commanded, "I adjure you demon to cease your torture of this child. By every name that is holy. I command you to be obedient or I will bind you with chains here and now and hold you for your just punishment of everlasting fire. By the Name of Jesus Christ of Nazareth, by the Name of Adoni, by the name of the unspeakable Tetragrammaton, by the Name of Father God, Creator of all things, I command you to cease and desist. By the fires that create and destroy, I command you. Lucifer was created by Father God and will be destroyed by Father God. All things have been given unto His Son, Christ Jesus, and I command you with the authority given to me by the Blood of that self-same Christ Jesus. I say stop! Cease!"

"Let's do this now, demon, now," James was shaking and his breathing was labored, but his voice was strong.

Sara's body turned and she stood on the cot. The horsehair blanket was in a pile on the floor. James was standing as well as he could, with the low roof, and his face nearly pressed against Sara's.

What Phyllis and Joselio saw was James with his face right in Sara's face, their foreheads nearly touching. Neither of them was moving, and this frozen state lasted for at least two hours. The temperature in the hut stabilized to normal. The candles and the lantern both relit by themselves. It was eerily quiet in the hut while both Phyllis and Joselio were trying to clear their minds. They then got down on their knees next to James, laid hands on him, and began to pray. What James was seeing was something totally different.

He was evidently in a spiritual realm of some kind. His mind was in overload and he was searching his memory for some guidance from the month of study: from the Bible, from his prayers, from somewhere..

In his mind James was praying, "God I need some help here, I really need some help here."

Chapter 20

James seemed to be standing in a very large room of sorts. He knew that he was in the mud hut on the side of Jefe Mountain, but at the same time he was somewhere else. The dimensions of the room were difficult to estimate, but the walls seemed to be hundreds of feet high for he could not see the ceiling. *He was reminded of the passage about the Mount of Transfiguration; when Peter, James and John were on the mountain here on earth, but right in front of them there were Elijah, Moses, Jesus and God speaking in the spiritual realm.* At first James thought the walls were moving, but upon closer observation it was as though lava was running down them. On two of the walls the lava ran down and on the other two walls it ran up. The lava was glowing fiery red with black crusty spots on the top or on the outside of the bright red parts. The floor could not be seen as there was a thick, ominous black fog about knee deep everywhere. The only sound was a creaking or groaning sound that reminded James of an old wooden ship he had once seen in a movie. It looked as though it should be extremely hot in the place, but the temperature seemed normal.

He sensed a presence and immediately responded to it, "I command you to show yourself Somne Octe. In the Name of Jesus, show yourself in your natural form. Now!"

A chariot appeared in front of James that was being pulled by a red horse. The chariot glowed so brightly that it looked as though it was made of molten metal. A large, well built, and strong looking individual that appeared in the shape of a human was in the Chariot and was holding a skull in his right hand and a large sword in his left. The being looked human, but James knew that it wasn't. This being was about the same size as the angel that had appeared on the oil lease four years earlier.

The one in the chariot spoke, "you challenged me, come and take your punishment!"

The scripture, *"not by might, not by power but by my Spirit says the Lord,"* came into James' mind.

He held his ground and spoke, "By that name above all names, the Name of Jesus, leave these mountains at once and never come back or you will be punished now. You will be bound in chains and held in the sumptuous pit until the day you will be cast into the lake of fire with all of your kind."

What took place then lasted for a long time, though James had no way of knowing how long. It was as though they were in a staring contest, like when he was a kid, and whoever blinked first lost.

Another scripture came to James' mind – *"for we wrestle not against flesh and blood but against principalities, against powers, against the rulers of the darkness of this age, against spiritual host of wickedness in the heavenly places."*

He began to repeat out loud the scriptures as the Holy Spirit brought them to his mind. He realized that he was speaking them in first person.

"Yet in all these things I am more than conquerors through Him who loves me. For I am persuaded that neither death nor life, nor angels nor principalities nor powers, nor things present nor things to come, nor height nor depth, nor any other created thing, shall be able to separate me from the love of God which is in Christ Jesus our Lord."

"And I saw something like a sea of glass mingled with fire and those who have the victory over the beast, over his image and over his mark and over the number of his name, standing on the sea of glass, having harps of God."

"Yes, even though I walk through the valley of the shadow of death, I will fear no evil; for you, God, are with me."

"And I will overcame him by the blood of the Lamb, Jesus, and by the word of my testimony, and I do not love my life to the death."

"These will make war with the Lamb, and the Lamb, Jesus, will overcome them, for He is Lord of lords and King of kings; and those who are with Him are called chosen and beautiful."

"The demons went up out of the pit and to the breadth of the earth; and surrounded the camp of the Saints and the beloved city. And fire came down from God out of heaven and devoured the demons and the devil, Lucifer, who deceived them, was cast into the lake of fire and brimstone where the beast and the false prophet are and they will be tormented day and night forever and ever."

"Now or later, Somne Octe, now or later, you will be punished for all eternity; do you want that punishment to start now or later?" James asked with the full authority of Heaven behind him. "Cease tormenting the girl and depart from here or your final fate will be brought on you here and now. You will be bound in chains now to wait on your final judgment. Now or later, Somne Octe, now or later!"

James then noticed there were two other figures behind Somne Octe. The first was sitting on a black horse and in his right hand held a large, long chain with locks on both ends. He was not overtly doing anything, just observing. He resembled Somne Octe in appearance and was very powerful looking. The Spirit of God revealed to James that this one was called Damian and he was the immediate superior of Somne Octe. The other being was standing off to the left observing all that was taking place. James just knew in his spirit who this was. The supreme evil one seemed to be about eight feet tall, handsome in appearance, carrying no weapons and wearing a robe. He looked for as though he was of Assyrian decent. He had medium length hair, down to the shoulders, with a full beard and an extremely stern and confident air about him. James knew that he was staring into the face of Lucifer himself, but surprisingly he felt no fear. All he felt was an urgent and determined purpose, a force driving him on and on.

Turning his attention back to Somne Octe and ordering him placed into bondage to await his final fate, James said, "By all the Names that God is called, by the Name of Jesus Christ, If you do not desist I will adjure, command, and cast you into the Pit to be held in chains."

Somne Octe was gone! The third being had spoken something that James did not understand and Somne Octe was just gone. The third being spoke again and Damien vanished before Jim's very eyes. James then turned and cast his gaze on this third being. Approximately ten feet separated them as they stared into each other's eyes. This impasse lasted for what seemed a very long time.

Then the Prince of Darkness spoke, "Another time, another place, you will be weak and you will pay dearly for what you and those you represent have wrought on my Kingdom. If you relate this instance to anyone, you will be severely dealt with for doing so. You will be mine, if not today, tomorrow, but you will be mine. I leave you now, but I will destroy you. You will not know when or how, but I will destroy you; I will make you forever regret coming to my mountains."

As quickly as he had appeared he was gone. James stood in the middle of the extremely large room and watched the lava flowing up and down the walls.

The tears began running down his face and he repeated over and over – "Thank you Jesus, thank you Jesus, thank you Jesus."

Phyllis and Joselio were still at their post in the mud hut, praying and laying hands on James. They could hear him speaking, but could not see or hear anyone else. For over two hours, he had not moved and they knew they were in a battle for his very life as well as Sara's and possibly their own. James then straightened up as well as he could, began rubbing his eyes and stretching his back and legs. They had become severely cramped over the last couple of hours. He retrieved a bottle of cola, drank it without stopping, had a second one, then a third. Then, totally ignoring Phyllis and Joselio, he sat down beside Sara who was now lying on the cot. He spoke to her and commanded the evil spirits that resided in her to depart. After convulsing her body, one left, coming out of her mouth, showing a really ugly apparition of himself and departing out the door. This was repeated over and over as the demons departed. Over two hundred times this occurred and the three Believers who were left in the mud hut on the side of that mountain saw the most grotesque and horrible looking beings any one could ever imagine. James realized that the demons presenting themselves in such horrid forms was the last ditch effort on the part of the demons to bring fear to the humans. The demons knew that they were defeated, that their command was in disarray, but they were still compelled to cause as much confusion and fear as possible.

After around two hours, the last of the demons departed Sara. Before it did, it caused many convulsions and much tearing to her body. There was a considerable amount of blood coming from her ears, nose, and mouth. After the last demon departed, Sara sat up with a very stupefied look on her face. She was totally confused. She then realized that she was naked in front of strangers and she was grabbing for something to cover herself. James looked away, as did Joselio, and James instructed his wife to cover her and then they would decide what to do next. Sara was free. She had been delivered. It had been forty-four and a half hours since the deliverance started, and it was now over.

James and Phyllis conferred on the next steps to take. He would have Joselio retrieve a bucket of water, some towels or rags, and water for Phyllis to bathe and dress the girl with the baptismal dress. Phyllis would also take care of a most important part of the deliverance. Sara had to hear and receive the Good News of the salvation of Jesus Christ.

James quoted the scripture that was applicable from the twenty-fourth verse of the eleventh chapter of Luke – *"When the unclean spirit goes out of a person, he goes into dry places, seeking rest; and finding none, he says, 'I will return to my house, the body from where I came', and if when he comes, he finds it empty, swept and in order, then he goes and takes with him seven other spirits more wicked that himself, and they enter and dwell there; and the last state of that person is worse that the first state."*

Sara must not be found empty but found to be a temple of the Spirit of the Living God. Joselio had brought a bucket of water from a horse trough that had not been destroyed the night before and Phyllis started to clean and care for the badly battered girl.

The American stepped outside the hut for the first time in nearly forty-five hours. He was fatigued beyond fatigue but was impervious to that fact. He stretched his legs and back and walked around standing up straight for the first time since he had entered the hut. It was still a little while before daylight, but the dawn would soon be breaking over the mountains. He surveyed the immediate area in the moonlight, the compound of the Soto family, and it looked like a bombed out village in the central highlands of Vietnam that he had once photographed. One of the huts was burned to the ground. Two others had burn damage. All of the fences had been torn down and the kicking of the horses and mules had caused much damage. The animals were gone, the family was gone, and the place looked deserted and abandoned. Turning his attention to the mud hut, James thought it was amazing that it was still standing. The roof was nearly half burned away. There were numerous holes dug into the dried mud sides where the dogs had attacked. The door was kicked off and in pieces on the ground, and many other areas had been damaged by animals, birds, and the elements. Three white doves sat peacefully, cooing on top of the hut. Joselio told James about the belief of the people in Mexico that black birds represent evil and white doves represent good, and that some of the people even believe the white doves are Angels from God.

On the side of the mountain, high above the village where Xanateo and his coven had been camping and watching the spectacle below, fear was rampant. They knew their leader had been humiliated. They knew the Prince would demote Somne Octe and they did not know what to do. They left for the cave where Sara had been indoctrinated to plan what to do to be restored to the favor of the powers of evil. They were rightfully afraid for it had been their responsibility to break the girl and to bring more hurt and confusion to the mountain. They had failed and they felt greatly concerned.

After a couple of hours, Joselio was sent to retrieve the aunt who had cared for Sara, and James went back into the hut. The stench was still there, the dampness was still there, and the darkness was still there, but that poor, wretched, demonic, possessed, and controlled girl was not. In place of that person was a gentle, pretty girl with a look of absolute amazement on her face. Sara sat on the stool that James had brought with him from Texas to use for the deliverance. She had on the white baptism dress that she had first worn two years previous. She was washed, her hair straightened up as much as possible, and she had a slight smile on her lips. She was terribly bruised with many burn marks and cuts, but she was free from the torment of the demons. James also noticed a ring on her right index finger that had not been there earlier; it was Phyllis' wedding ring. Phyllis related later that the Spirit had spoken to her to give the ring to Sara so she would feel beautiful about herself. As instructed, she did not place it on the marriage hand, but rather on the index finger of the right hand. Sara seemed to be in a mild stupor but she did not seem to have an excessive amount of pain, especially for all the damage that had been done to her by the hurtful demons.

The first words she spoke to James were in her own voice and in Spanish, "Thank you, thank you, it is over, yes?"

"Yes, Sara, it is over, you are free of the evil that had control of you," James responded.

The old Evangelist, Joselio, came back to the compound with Sara's aunt. The aunt was absolutely beside herself with joy and gratefulness. She kept waving her arms in the air and praising God, and then she would fall down on her knees and start praying, then jump up and start waving her arms again. She ran over to James and started kissing the back of his hand. He was taken back by the action until Joselio explained that it was a local custom and a sign of extreme respect, most often used by grandchildren toward their grandfather. The aunt was then given instructions as to the care of Sara.

"Do not let the immediate family come around her," James told the faithful relative. "They have not yet decided how to deal with this, so it is up to you. In thirty days, I will return and spend time with Sara until we will decide what must be done next. Nourish her, love her, read the New Testament to her every day, and pray, pray, pray."

The aunt led the shaky girl away to her own compound to do as instructed. Joselio was then requested to help in any way possible to aid in the girl's recovery, and he readily agreed. He would make a camp above the aunt's compound and watch over the girl's recovery. Joselio seemed to know that there could be both spiritual and physical danger for Sara, and he would be there for any problems. After taking one last survey of the hut where Sara had been and the utter destruction of the compound, James and his wife started down the steep side of the mountain towards the lower part of the village.

The village had come to life as the sun rose over the mountains. The inhabitants were scurrying around; fixing what had been broken during the chaos. The animosity of the day before that was focused on the Americans was gone. The confusion caused by the demons had vanished. It was just another day on the side of the Jefe Mountain. The resilience of these wonderful mountain inhabitants would never cease to amaze the couple from the States. The villagers had survived many disasters over the past two hundred years and this one was taken in stride. The couple went to the small church building with the dirt floor, made pallets, lay down and, after a heartfelt prayer of gratitude, slept for nearly ten hours.

When they awoke, they found the villagers had prepared food for them and it was consumed with great joy and much gusto. As they were preparing to leave in the late afternoon, they were given many handmade gifts: small pottery water containers, needle–crafts, and other things. Although the Americans were definitely planning on returning soon, the people insisted on many very firm promises that they would return and the exact date of that return. Later, as they drove down the mountain, they joined in prayer to thank God for everything that had taken place. They thanked Him especially for His love toward His people, His creation, His Son, His Holy Spirit, and for deliverance from evil. On the way down the mountain and then out of the valley to the desert below, they saw many white doves sitting on fence post and flying overhead. On the way to Jefe Mountain, they had seen no white doves, only the black ravens. James thought that maybe there was something to that local old wives tale about the white doves and the black birds.

Chapter 21

One month later.

The climb up the mountain on this trip was considerably easier than the ones before. They were in a four-wheel-drive van they had purchased. The high clearance, large motor, transmission cooler, double duty radiator, etc. made navigating the steep trail quite easy; though the vehicle's climbing ability did little to overcome the narrowness of that small road. As they pulled into the village, the beauty of the place overwhelmed James and Phyllis again. This would happen each time they arrived there, no matter how many hundreds of times they arrived over the years. To say that the welcome by the villagers was warm would be a gross understatement. The village as a whole was ecstatic that the Americans had returned. They spent two weeks on the mountain this trip, holding services and visiting with a well-recuperated Sara. James also had time for a long, sincere visit with Joselio, who had made his small camp above the compound, overlooking the hut where Sara was now staying. Joselio had sat there all day, every day, for a month, watching and praying. James was still amazed about this old preacher. Each of the different families offered their kitchen huts as a place to visit in and to eat, and eat and eat. With all the eating and visiting going on, James knew it would be diet time when they returned back to Texas. Many came to know the Lord on this visit and great rejoicing took place for each of them – there on Jefe Mountain and also on the Holy Mountain in Heaven.

The time spent with Sara astounded James. She was well spoken, not bashful as most of the villagers her age were. She readily revealed to the Americans, in great detail, the things that she had suffered at the hands of the Warlock, the Witches and the demons. Some of the things she told would not be believed by most, but with what James and Phyllis had gone through the month before, their believing it was never a problem. She related about the forced violation and sodomy, the séances, the fortune telling, her familiar spirits, and finally the total possession. Amazingly, she remembered each demon by its name and by the time that it came to take residence in her. She also had vivid memories of the particular torture that each demon brought with it. She recalled most of the deliverance with the viewpoint of being on the inside looking out versus being on the outside looking in.

Sara wanted permission to tell everyone so that they could be aware of the dangers of having any dealings with the evil ones. James told her it was fine for her to share with the villagers about the danger of dealing with the brujas, but cautioned her not to speak to the other villagers about the sexual abuses or the deeper spiritual things. He made many pages of notes and tape recordings of Sara recounting the events of that terrible ordeal. The depths of pain, torture, and degradation the girl had been put through physically sickened him. He knew that she was not the only one to suffer this, but just one of thousands or even millions under the power of the enemy. Maybe most of them were not controlled to the extent that Sara was, but he believed that bondage was bondage. Sara was no longer a captive of the enemy, she was free.

"I have come to set at liberty those who are captive," from the very beginning of the ministry of Jesus Christ, appropriately described Sara's liberation.

The two weeks passed very quickly. As James and Phyllis were preparing to leave, two events took place. Joselio told James that he would be leaving to go to another place where he was needed. How Joselio knew that he was needed was a mystery to all, as he had had no contact with anyone outside the village. He told everyone good-bye and walked off toward the peak of Jefe Mountain. Neither James nor anyone in San Mateo ever saw or heard from him again.

Thinking about Joselio over the years, James and Phyllis often considered the scripture in Hebrews' thirteenth chapter – *"Do not forget to entertain strangers, for by so doing some have unwittingly entertained angels."* Maybe James and Phyllis had entertained an angel.

The second thing that happened was a request from the Mayor not to leave just yet, as they were having a town meeting, and it concerned James and his family. All the families met together with the exception of Sara's immediate family. That family had been asked, but they refused to come. James and Phyllis waited for what seemed like forever and then the villagers came back to the vehicle. There were telling smiles on many faces, but James could not figure out what the smiles were telling. The Mayor, with much fanfare, told the Americans that the village was communally owned by the decedents of the founders. Many of the descendents of the founders had fought and many of them had died in the early 1900s for the right to own the land. That was during the revolution of Pancho Villa that had started around 1913. Since that time, no one except the families of the heroes who fought and gave their lives in the revolution and the survivors of that revolution had lived here.

That day the village had voted to ask James, Phyllis, and their children, to become members and residents of the village. This included a place to build a dwelling (a compound area) and the right to farm, ranch, or otherwise use the thousands of acres that were part of village. This would also include the right to vote in the town meetings. "Would you accept this offer?" the Mayor inquired with much pomp and fan-fair. James replied, without much consideration, that it would be their honor to be part of the village for as long as God would permit them. He told them that he would move down in a few months, but that he would be back each month until the final move. He would accept the area to build a compound, but had no need for use of the farming or ranching area, as his work was to be in the spiritual realm. The Mayor informed James that, as a member of the Ejido (commune), he would be required to spend time watching the communally owned animals, working on the roads, and repairing the town meeting building. This was the customary exchange of work for the use of some of the land. James replied that he would do his required share of the communal work, but that he would not expect anything in exchange and that the plan was for him to live part of the time in Texas and part of the time in Mexico. When he was there on the mountain, he would do his full month's allotment of work and therefore be an equal shareholder in the Ejido. After much fanfare and many hugs and handshakes, the good-byes were said and the Americans headed back to Texas.

About half-way back to Texas (time-wise), the couple stopped in the relatively large city of Victoria. They made some phone calls back to the States, and after sufficient arrangements had been made, including a longer stay in Mexico, they went to a secluded "Hide-a-Way" of a lodge that was owned by some members of their church in Texas. The Lodge was in the mountains at the south end of the city. Access was only by driving six miles along a shallow riverbed through the canyons, which was only accessible during dry weather. The place was marvelous, with one elderly caretaker and his wife, and it was quiet, secluded, and very comfortable. They were the only ones staying at the Lodge, and all the cooking of the food, laundry, etc. was handled by the caretaker and his wife, Francisco and Maria. James and Phyllis spent one full week at this wonderfully beautiful and secluded spot, praying, resting, listening to God, and making plans for their future in Mexico.

The conversations and plans they had made over the past few months were always to minister to the people of Mexico on a part-time basis. James had built a relatively successful pest control company in south Texas. He and his wife had always felt that they would oversee the business for a month or so and then go to Mexico for a week or two, and repeat the cycle. They'd have the best of both worlds: being foreign Missionaries and living a comfortable lifestyle in the United States. That seemed like an absolutely reasonable plan for the family. They would soon learn that God's ways are not necessarily our ways, and many plans that man might devise just do not work out they way they were planned to work out.

During the retreat and seclusion of that week, God spoke to both James and Phyllis; and He did this many times and in great detail. They were instructed to sell the business, sell their home, leave their church and friends, and to take their two children and their dog and move to Mexico. They were not to be concerned about how they were going to make the move, or how they were going to support themselves. They were only to be obedient to the instructions and go forth. James got the worn map of Mexico from the vehicle and, as he prayed, God had him mark twenty-four places on that map with an X. He wrote on the map as instructed, and he wrote "churches to be established." Every mark was in a blank area on the map. Some were in the desert area of Central Mexico, some in the jungle area of the Yucatan, and some in the mountainous areas. Not one of these places had a road to it indicated on the map or a name by the location. The scope and importance of the calling for the family was almost too much for James, but he knew that if God had called it to be, it would be. They decided that when they returned to Mexico they would first go back to San Mateo and minister to Sara, and learn what they could about the evilness of the dark side so they could put that information out for public consumption.

Chapter 22

Upon their return to Texas, they told their children that they were moving to Mexico to be Missionaries. There was a fair amount of excitement with the children; the prospects of living in a strange land, and not having to go to a formal school, were well received. Then they visited the Pastor of the church where they were members. They received some good counsel, but not a lot of encouragement for "just up and moving to Mexico." The decision was made to discuss it in more detail at a future date, "after you have had time to calm down from all the excitement." James did not let the discouragement detour him in the least, and he continued on with the plans as he and Phyllis had discussed and prayed about at the Lodge.

When the steps were made to sell the business and the house, the business broker and the real estate agent both threw up the same road blocks. They both wanted a few months to get the best deal on the business and property. James informed them that they had less than three weeks to close the sales or he would give the property and the business to the first person he met on the street. Since there would be no commissions if James gave the business and property away, they got busy and found buyers. As with all start-up businesses and newer purchased homes, the equity did not produce any profit. When all was said and done, James and his family had less that two thousand dollars left over.

They went back to their Pastor to talk more about the move to Mexico. The Pastor was no more supportive than he was before. He did offer James an associate Pastor's position and promised to consider the move to Mexico in a year. James flatly refused and retold the Pastor what God had done in the mountains of Mexico, and what instructions God had given them at the Lodge. After much prayer, the Pastor said that if they were that determined to go to Mexico, then so be it; they would have his and the church's blessings. This was a major hurdle to clear for James strongly believed that he had to be sent out with the blessings and with the accountability that accompanied that blessing.

The day they were getting ready to leave, the Pastor and the Board of the Church told James that they would donate the evening offering from the last Sunday of the month to the effort. That particular offering had been averaging approximately one hundred dollars per month. After supplies, school material for home schooling the children, and miscellaneous other Items were bought, and as they crossed the border into Mexico, James and Phyllis were debt free. In the van were James, Phyllis, two daughters ages six and eight, one large Chesapeak Retriever, everything they owned in the world, two hundred and eighty three dollars, and the pledge of the last offering of the month from their home church. They were on a mission for God, and nothing would hold them back. Or at least that is what they fully believed.

The men from the church that owned the Lodge in Mexico had asked James and his family to please spend some time there on the way to the interior of Mexico. They had gladly accepted and late the first night of their travels they pulled into the secluded and beautiful lodge. They were greeted by Francisco and

Maria, who quickly blurted that after James had left three weeks earlier, they had considered the Gospel that was shared and had become Christians. There was great rejoicing and while the couple's daughters and the dog explored the shallow river and surrounding mountains, James and Phyllis prayed, discussed plans, and prepared for the great adventure ahead.

They considered the twenty-four Xs on the map and wondered what was ahead of them at each one. After the events of the last few months, there was no doubt that each mark on that map would bring forth great and mighty things. They knew that each mark represented a future building and, more importantly, people who would become Christians and meet in those buildings. In actuality they were just marks on a piece of paper, but in the minds and spirits of the James' each held the promise of a new adventure; lost and dying people who needed the Good News of Christ, and another opportunity to be obedient to God.

One area that they spent a lot of time considering was the prospect of dealing with what to do with Sara. Sara could relate to them so much about the other side, the evil side of the spiritual realm. While in the States, James had contacted the publisher of 'Charisma Magazine', a Christian monthly publication. They had discussed the possibility of doing a story on Sara, concentrating on the time of her possession, and the spiritual aspects of that possession. Over the years James had read a number of accounts of demonic possession, but they just did not ring with the sincerity with which Sara spoke. There had also been conversations with some of the new cable televisions Christian shows about bringing Sara to the States for interviews; or at least video taping interviews with her in Mexico and integrating the interviews into programs to be aired on the networks.

James and Phyllis were very excited about all these prospects. Excited to be able to show, not tell, but show people the depths to which the devil will go to fulfill his duties to steal, kill, and destroy. It seemed that most Believers in Christianity just did not accept that the stories related in Scripture about demonic possession were true, and the ones that did believe the Biblical stories were true, rejected the notion that they still took place. James felt that the devil had done a great job of confusing folks about this real and present danger to people. This had been accomplished by convincing those people that evil was some kind of mental defect, and not an organized controlled force of evil that permeated every culture.

They discussed what Scripture said in Matthew about following Christ;

Matt 16:24. Then Jesus said to His disciples, "If anyone desires to come after Me, let him deny himself, and take up his cross, and follow Me. For whoever desires to save his life will lose it, but whoever loses his life for My sake will find it."

James and Phyllis had lost the life they had known, taken up the Cross of Jesus, and found true life and the true deep spiritual meaning of that life. All the goals and plans that they had made during the first few years of their marriage were just distant memories. The desire to one day become financially successful, to own a large home in an upper-class neighborhood, and to be respected for accomplishments of success in the business world all meant absolutely nothing to them now. They only wanted to serve the people that God would bring into their path. Their thoughts all centered on doing something for someone else, no matter what sacrifice it would take to accomplish it. They were so excited to get started, to build a life in Mexico, to learn the customs of the people, and to get to know Sara and learn more about her and all the things she could relate to benefit others. Chapter 23

As they entered the edge of the village of San Mateo, it was obvious that something was wrong. Only one of the original Christians had walked down to meet them. His face was solemn and his words were barely audible as he greeted James and his family.

After the customary greeting and hugs, he blurted out in Spanish, "Sara, si murio!" Sara is dead.

James asked for him to repeat what he had said; it was the same, Sara was dead. He heard the words, but his mind wanted to reject them. Surely this was some kind of sad joke and the man would smile any minute and say, "Let's go see Sara." Sara was probably behind one of the huts watching to see what their reaction would be. It was going to be like a surprise party, where everyone runs out and says, "Surprise, Happy Birthday!" It simply had to be something such as that; it just couldn't be true that Sara was dead. James soon realized that it was not a joke, and the seriousness of his greeter was more than telling. It was as though a giant tree had fallen on James and crushed him. It was a few moments before he could even form a thought about what to do or say next.

"Sara is dead. Sara is dead. Sara is dead. That is not supposed to be. That is not in the plan. That can't have happened. It just can't," James thought as his mind raced and rebelled at what he was hearing.

After the walk up the mountain to where the aunt's huts were located, and after drinking the required cup of coffee offered to him by the aunt, he inquired as to what had taken place.

Sara had continued to improve for two weeks. She spent much time visiting with the other families in the village, openly sharing the parts of what had taken place that were appropriate. She warned people about the dangers of dealing with the Warlock and his Witches. As Jim had instructed it was not prudent for her to talk of the sexual abuses, though most of the villagers probably had a good idea what had taken place. Then, one morning about two weeks past, Sara's father came to the aunt to ask if Sara could please come and visit her immediate family. He stated that they wanted things to be back as they used to be. The aunt did not think she could refuse; after all, there had been no sign of trouble from the family. Sara put on her baptism dress to look as nice as she could for her family, and went with her father. The truth behind the visit would not be apparent to Sara or her aunt until it was too late to avoid the pending dangers.

The night before, while the village was quiet and sleeping, Xanateo and his four witches had quietly and secretly came to the parents' compound. They convinced the family that they had to bring Sara to Xanateo or great problems would befall all the family. It didn't take a lot of convincing, since the family was still extremely shameful of the whole situation and fearful of the Warlock and his witches. When Sara arrived at the family's compound, she was physically forced into what was left of the mud hut, the same place where she had spent so much horrible time. Xanateo's plan had been to get Sara to renounce her faith in Christ and join the Coven once again. This would please the evil demonic powers and limit the punishment that Xanateo knew was going to befall his Coven. They talked with Sara for hours with promises of fame, fortune, and recognition. Sara responded that she held no ill will or hatred towards them and that she only wanted her village to be free of the evil. When the Warlock and the Witches failed on that front, they threatened her with more of the same punishment that she had suffered the night of her indoctrination. Sara's response was that she was now a child of God and nothing they could do would bring harm to her.

Finally, out of desperation, the Witches held her down and started trying to put curses on her; commanding her to renounce her new faith and the God in whom she had found faith. Sara was told that she must tell the villagers that the American Missionary had given money to her to lie about what had happened to her. The Witches while holding Sara down had tried to force her to drink the potions of drugs that they had prepared. Sara was held against her will for over six hours. Xanateo took the obsidian stone knife that had been used to cut the pentagram in her chest and threatened to cut one in her face if she did not agree. She told them she was not afraid, for the Angels of God would protect her. Some of the other villagers realized that something bad was happening, but the code of the mountains kept them from interfering in the internal family affair of another family. A few drew close to the compound as they had done when the Americans was there praying for Sara, but there was no help for Sara.

Xanateo screamed that the only way they were going to get her to come back would be the same way as before. He ordered the witches to tear her clothes off and hold her down on the cot, and he would again rape and sodomize her. The thought of raping someone who was not a virgin and not so young anymore repulsed him, but the situation had made him desperate. Xanateo began to disrobe as three of the Witches held Sara down and the fourth began ripping her clothes. Sara jerked her arms loose and stood up, but did not fight the abusers. She raised both hands above her head as far as she could and shouted, "Alabanza al Dios, alabanza al Dios, alabanza al Dios," (Praise God, praise God, praise God). She shouted over and over at the top of her voice. The villagers could hear Sara praising God and they were confused about what was going on in the mud hut. It was not the intention of the Warlock for Sara to die, but die she did, right in the middle of one of her praises to God. Sara fell straight back, landing solidly on the floor, and was dead before she even reached the floor. Xanateo and the Witches ran from the hut and climbed over the fence. Under a hail of rocks thrown by the few villagers who had came close to the compound, the Warlock and his Coven fled down the mountain.

It was the next day before the aunt asked the family if she could please see about Sara. As she approached the doorway, somehow she knew that thing were not right. As the aunt looked inside the mud hut she saw Sara on her back. Her white baptismal dress had been ripped from her shoulders and down the side, and yet it still covered her. She appeared as though she was asleep, very peaceful, and with a slight smile on her lips. The expression on her face was as though she had seen something absolutely wonderful just before she died. Her arms were stretched as far as they could be, straight above her head, and her hands and fingers were also extended to their full length. The aunt respectfully backed out of the hut, went to the few Christians that were at the fence, and told them of what she saw. They began to pray and sing praises to God. Later that day, an agreement was made with the family by the Christians for the Christians to bury Sara. They gathered what lumber they could to make a casket, but there was a problem when they came to measure Sara.

It had been more than sufficient time for Sara's body to go through the stiffening stage and become limp again, but her arms could not be moved. The arms were frozen in the upward stretching position with the hands and fingers still outstretched. The only way her arms could have been pulled down and crossed over her chest in the customary burial position would be to break her shoulder joints, elbows, and wrists. No one was willing to desecrate the body so she could be placed in the customary burial position. After much discussion, they decided to make the coffin to accommodate the raised arms. It was the longest coffin ever made on the side of Jefe Mountain. Before the burial the next day, the word spread throughout the mountains about the girl who died praising God, and who was still praising God even in death.

The funeral was held at the small church with the dirt floor early the next morning, and Sara was buried at mid-day. Bodies were not embalmed in the mountains and had to be buried quickly. Even with the rushed time frame for the burial, it was estimated that well over a thousand people walked or rode their animals to be a part of the event; to see the girl who praised God even in death. As was the custom, Sara's casket was taken to the graveyard on a drag sled pulled behind a horse. The casket lids were customarily left off on the crude wooden caskets so the onlookers could have one last glimpse of the departed. Then the lids would be put on just before interment. As Sara was taken down the rough trail to the place of her burial, every time the sled went over a particularly rough spot, her body would rock in the casket and her stiff arms would sway back and forth. This movement was accented by the flash of the diamond ring on her right hand that Phyllis had given the girl. The onlookers were somewhat frightened, though totally enthralled by this spectacle. She praised God all the way to the graveyard. Sara became known as "The girl who praised God even in death," and the story spread, and still spreads, throughout those mountains.

James felt really sick to his stomach as he walked up past the compound that contained the mud hut. He went on, up to the mountain to the large rock where he had prayed before starting the deliverance of Sara. He would grow to know that place very well over the ensuing years. It was a place where he would talk to God and God would respond to him. He sat down on the large flat rock and looked out over the valley below. James opened his Bible and read for a little while, trying to find solace, but finding that solace was impossible and he could not reconcile the confusion in his mind. He closed the Bible and looked out over the tremendously beautiful terrain. The extremely large mountains, deep valleys, and beautiful blue sky with just a few small white clouds caused him to think this place really was heaven on earth. But he just didn't feel like he belonged there, or actually anywhere, at this juncture of his life. James was hurting so very badly, and the hurt was coming from way down, deep inside of him, overwhelming him, consuming him.

With tears streaming down his face, James looked upward and spoke, at first his voice was quivering and then began to break up as he cried out, "God, why? Why? My beloved Savior, why all this that has happened, and now she is gone. I do not understand this God, I just flat-out plain do not understand this."

As James sat on the rock and looked at towards the heavens he saw many different colors that resembled a kaleidoscope display, and as the colors seemed to fill the sky; he got his answer.

The answer to his question was quick and firm, "My ways are not your ways. Understand this; Sara pleased Me and I brought her home. Do you understand that? Sara pleased **Me** and **I** brought her home."

James felt a shudder that began deep down in his soul, in the center of his very being. He began weeping as he had never thought possible. He sat there for a long while with his shoulders and chest heaving, tears streaming down his face and pouring onto the rock, as knowledge was put into his heart by the Spirit of God. Sara had accomplished what all believers should desire to do: to please God and be taken into His presence. No wonder Sara had that pleased look on her face when she had died. She saw behind the curtain at what was waiting for her. She pleased God and He took her home! Hallelujah to the Lamb of God. She pleased God and He took her home!

Epilog

Sara's family moved from the village and never returned. Though the family had been on this mountain for generations, the shame was too much for them to bear and continue to live there. They are carrying their burden somewhere, but no one on the mountain knows exactly where.

Somne Octe was demoted completely and banished to the grotto area of the northern mountains. Somne Octe was ordered by his superiors to exist in dry places or to enter only the coyotes or other animals of that remote area. He was forbidden by Damian to ever enter a human again, based on his failure with Sara. Somne Octe meanwhile blamed Xanateo and the Coven of Witches for his failures.

Josefa, one of the Witches, came to James about a year after Sara's death and converted to Christianity. She then moved to San Mateo and spent the rest of her life helping those to whom she had brought so much misery. She spent untold hundreds of hours over the years sharing with the American and revealing to him all of the dark secrets of evil that she had spent over sixty years learning. One important thing she did for this book was to share the conversations that had taken place among the demons during the Sara's ordeal. She had been made privy to these, as the entire Coven had been and she related Sara's last moments before she died. Josefa also gave James all of the ancient manuscripts, amulets, and writings that she had been entrusted with, teaching him how to interpret the cuneiform and other strange markings. She lived 17 years in servitude to the village of San Mateo, and when she died she received a Christian burial with hundreds of grateful people attending.

James and his family built a place to live in San Mateo with the required thatched roof. They spent over seven years living among the wonderful people of the mountains and traveling to other areas of Mexico. When the time came for them to move back to the States, and on to other areas of the world, twenty-four churches had been established and over three thousand people were devoted church attendants and Christians. All of the Xs on the map, which James always had close by, had been replaced with crosses representing churches that had been established. After spending a total of 20 years as missionaries in Mexico, Central/South America, The Philippines, and Indonesia (on the islands of Timor and Sumatra), James and Phyllis are now Pastors in the United States

Joselio, the old itinerate preacher, has not been heard from, so you decide: was he an Angel or just an old Preacher? Either way, James and Phyllis will always have a wonderful place in their hearts for him and their encounter.

The Mayor leads the singing at the vibrant small church in San Mateo.

The Mayor's son is a full-time Evangelist in southern Mexico. He is taking the Gospel to the State of Chiapas.

Ramon and his group in San Bastian are still running shotgun for the drug trade and spreading fear wherever they can. Their practice of Santeria has gotten more gruesome as time passes.

Pancho Rameriz, the very large, retarded giant of a young man that brutalized Sara so severely, came to an evangelistic meeting James was holding and asked for prayer. He was saved, totally healed of his retardation syndrome, and is very active in the local church in his village. He is living a productive and fulfilling Christian life.

San Mateo Cemetery is high on the side of Jefe Mountain, and the locals still talk of the grave of the girl who praised God even in death. Many make the trek to see the gravesite that is longer than any other there. They stand in wonder at the site, but will they ever truly understand the events that transpired on this mountain? Sometimes people talk of a very large giant of a man walking over the mountains to the remote cemetery, kneeling, praying, and leaving freshly picked flowers on the grave of the girl that praised God even in death.

The four Rameriz brothers, after seeing the miracle that happened to their younger brother, came to an outdoor meeting James held in their town. They were saved and converted to Christianity. They repented for their evil ways and went back to the family tradition of growing corn, instead of marijuana. They are also raising their respective families according to Christian principles.

The Laguna Church is growing steadily. James found them a younger, single Pastor who dedicated his life to teaching the Gospel in that area. He married the young woman, Juanita, and (at last count) they had five children. The noise of the wind does not sound when they pray, and the road is still not finished over the mountains to El Lemon.

Xanateo and two of his witches, Brillentina and Magdelena, as they were passing through a remote high pass on the way to recruit another young girl, were mauled to death by a rabid mountain lion in the grotto area of the northern mountains. Others traveling in the group said a large mountain lion that was foaming at the mouth came out of nowhere and tore the three to pieces. The rabid mountain lion did not attack or even notice any of the other twenty or so travelers. This was the same area to which Somne Octe was banished.

Santiaga, the Witch, moved to Monterrey, Mexico, and still pursues her evil trade as a Santeria Priestess among the uninformed. She has been elevated to high Priestess of the area in the practice of Santeria, and she still make holds Santeria meeting in San Bastian.

Lucifer is still the Prince of the power of the air and lord of this earth until Jesus returns. He is still controlling those he can, still hurting those he can, and still killing those he can. It is a battle out there, and you can only win if you are on the right side and use the right weapons.

Printed in the United States
206975BV00001B/1-24/P

9 781593 305505